WHERE ANGELS DARE

Angelwalk Series

Where Angels Dare

Roger Elwood

Broadman & Holman Publishers
Nashville, Tennessee

0-8054-1877-6

Published by Broadman & Holman Publishers, Nashville, Tennessee
Acquisitions and Development Editor: Leonard G. Goss
Page Design and Typesetting: PerfecType, Nashville, Tennessee

Dewey Decimal Classification: 813
Subject Heading: NOVEL
Library of Congress Card Catalog Number: 98-48385

Library of Congress Cataloging-in-Publication Data

Elwood, Roger.
Where angels dare / Roger Elwood.
p. cm.
ISBN 0-8054-1877-6
I. Title.
PS3555.L85W48 1999
813'.54--dc21

98-48385
CIP

3 4 5 03 02 01 00 99

DEDICATION

Dot Conover
—who helped to
make it all possible

Want is a growing giant which the coat of
Have was never large enough to cover.

Ralph Waldo Emerson

PROLOGUE

He is not poor that hath not much,
but he that craves much.

Thomas Fuller

Angels were regularly being sent by God to do their work on Planet Earth. Most of the time, they were without any form—invisible but real—gently prodding people—adjutants to their consciences, introducing a thought, a desire, a noble aspiration. It had been this way since soon after Adam and Eve were dismissed from the garden of Eden.

The unfallen angels were the benevolent and quite beautiful messengers of God's wishes and will, forever obedient to Him, forever eager to please their Creator by helping His mortal creations.

But—

There were others.

Also angels.

But fallen, willful, disobedient, banned forever from the presence of the Almighty, messengers not of God, but hapless slaves to their own master, dark and unholy and evil as he was and ever would be.

Satan.

That the former archangel Lucifer did exist could be easily seen by witnessing all the evil in the world, wickedness in high and low places.

A war for souls was in progress on Planet Earth—and gambling was one of the weapons.

Eden . . . once blessed Eden.

Just then, Darien was remembering the original, utterly faultless state of Eden, those moments during which he and God had been with the first humans, enjoying a blissful communion that was surpassed only by that which He enjoyed with the Son and the Holy Spirit in heaven.

Sublime . . .

That was the only word that could convey the state of life in Eden. No animals had to be killed for food, no skins worn as coats or jackets. Disease did not exist. There was no hunger, no fear, only supreme goodness.

And no crime.

Rape was not known. Stealing, murder, lying . . . these did not intrude.

"How sad!" Darien exclaimed, filled with a sorrow that shook the cosmos. "How sad that they would not listen, would not heed!"

Though of spirit and not flesh-and-blood body, this angel and all other unfallen ones knew the greatest of happiness, knew the most profound of sorrow, knew exultation as well as despair.

They could laugh, could cry.

God gave little to His human creations that He Himself did not possess, except His divinity.

And it was the same with His angels.

And Darien, an unfallen angel, did not find it difficult to agree with his Creator, having himself been a part of Eden and, after the Fall, a frequent visitor there to commiserate with the angel assigned to guarding the entrance so that no mortal or demon would enter it until the time of the new heaven and the new earth.

"I know how you feel," Darien said as he stood with Stedfast, another unfallen angel. "Eden was so perfect."

Perfect . . .

It was that.

Animals never killed for food. Trees stayed strong and healthy. The air was always clean. Water utterly pure.

No factories, no assembly plants, no chemical wastes—nothing at all that needed to be made because Eden was wholly self-sufficient unto itself and for the needs of every human being.

Eden was not to have been a single place.

Eden was intended to be constantly growing, developing, like a gigantic single living organism, to cover the entire surface of Planet Earth, to make that world the garden spot of all of galactic creation. As more human beings were to be born, they would obey God's laws not of a slavishness that made them little more than ventriloquists' dummies but of a *desire* to do so, since pleasing Him gave them the most ecstatic of pleasures.

That was what had been intended—Eden, the center of a planet that was the center of the universe.

Gone.

Ended.

Finished.

"It was . . . as you say," replied Stedfast, appreciating the other angel's sensitivity, but then this had been typical of Darien since he had commenced his odyssey along the eternal path called Angelwalk, starting at the throne upon which the Creator sat and ending on the planet raped by Satan and tens of thousands of fellow fallen angels.

"A touch of heaven," Stedfast added.

"More than that."

Stedfast looked at his comrade quizzically.

"More than a mere touch of heaven, my friend . . . rather it was an *extension* of our home here."

Darien's awareness was brightened and he could see so clearly what God meant by those words when He birthed the thought.

"I understand that now, of course."

"They gave them perfection," Stedfast said, sharing in the revelation.

"And the first human beings turned it into—"

Darien the angel could not continue, his memories all too fresh because in heaven, clocks and calendars and the frame of reference they embodied did not exist, and what had been centuries of time on Planet Earth were just equivalent "days" eternally.

That Adam and Eve paid the price of their rebellion was one thing but that left behind them the tragic wreckage of what could have been.

Total peace. Total joy. Total freedom from disease.

Giving up that third area, the state of remarkable health enjoyed by Adam and Eve was the worst of the punishments suffered, bringing into the world system all the cancers, viruses, other causes of pain and suffering in every country in every age of the history of the Human Race.

"Dear Stedfast, to see how many methods my human creations have tried or been searching for as they blindly pursue finding the way back to Eden is so pathetic," God spoke again.

"Because people always go the wrong way," Stedfast added forlornly. "It is in their nature. A lie they can make up, a lie they can *pretend* is real, yet it does not abolish the truth as it stands there before them."

They both had been looking down at Planet Earth and surveying its present state, determined not to shrink back from what God saw.

In Bosnia, they saw the unmarked graves of thousands of men, women, and children who were slaughtered for the sake of the Nazi-like scourge of ethnic cleansing. In Africa, countless numbers of men, women, and children were dying of hunger or because they were on what happened to be the wrong political side—or was *thought* to be. In China, protesting students were gunned down for exercising a freedom that existed even in the Soviet Union. In Chicago and Los Angeles, people were beaten by police simply because their black skin made them seem suspicious.

Darien assumed that his next assignment would be in one of *those* places, to attend to the needs of the dying, to minister in whatever possible way to the living.

Despite his experience, despite his depiction, he, as an angel, was not perfect. Only God had that distinction. Nor was he all-knowing. Again, that was the Creator's province. And he had just made the mistake of forgetting, however briefly, that those in greatest need, spiritually, were not always in the midst of a war or a siege of famine or disease.

They could be in palaces of marble and gold fixtures and rare tapestries and all the other embellishments of wealth.

"There," both angels were told as God indicated a particular area on earth. "That is where I want you to go, Darien—you and Stedfast."

Darien was becoming excited since, in the past, he had had to work alone. Having the companionship of another angel would prove, he was sure, a not insignificant blessing.

"It is terribly unfortunate," Stedfast suggested, "you know, seeing what we do of all the evil and the sin that mankind commits."

"Yes, it is," the angel replied.

"Greed, you know. That is at the root of a great deal of it. Has not greed been the root of many of the crimes of history, greed for land, greed for money?"

They both lapsed into a certain quiet briefly because they had seen *all* of history, seen battlefields with blood inches deep, seen husbands betray their wives, people robbed, pain and suffering throughout time for just one compelling motivation, one perpetual obsession.

"The *love* of money," Stedfast went on.

"You are right. Money has become a veritable god of sorts. It is the focus of entire sections of newspapers across the nation. Greed propels swindles and scams and other schemes. Those obsessed by money try to deceive themselves into thinking that having money is a necessity. That in itself may be considered prudent. But so many *need* it because they have plunged themselves into heavy levels of debt. For some, gambling seemed to offer a marvelous answer."

"Is that not true everywhere?"

"But never more so than there."

They knew that God was guiding them toward a certain spot as He directed their attention accordingly.

"Las Vegas?" Darien asked.

He could not discern from the flickering lights below exactly what state or city was involved.

"You asked about Las Vegas, Darien," God spoke.

"Why, Father?"

"They have great need, those who live and work in Las Vegas or simply visit it from time to time."

"I would not have thought it otherwise."

Darien had passed through Las Vegas more than once. The glitter of so many colorful lights was beguiling. But what happened when there was a power shortage? Darkness engulfed Las Vegas. There were good people in and around the town, ministries dedicated to saving souls for Christ, noble people, decent and selfless, but they were submerged in a morass of greed and materialism.

Darien spoke of this to Stedfast as God remained quiet for a bit.

"Many of the people running Las Vegas are plugged into the wrong master," he said. "The rest are mindless dupes. They should be pitied rather than loathed."

"That they are. And that I feel, pity for the puppets who do not even know that someone is pulling their strings."

"When Armageddon is being fought, Satan will forget about this place and rally all his troops for that final conflict."

"And Las Vegas will be in darkness."

"As it is now but without the fake joy."

"God wants us to minister here, to lead some of the people into the only light that counts."

But God interrupted. "No, Darien, I do not."

"Oh?"

"Look over there," God said, pointing to the right of Las Vegas.

"Yes, Father, what is it that you want me to see?"

"Another place. It represents a great deal, you know, for it signifies the spread of this evil beyond the confines of Las Vegas, as the beginning of an assault upon the mainstream of American life."

"A place like Las Vegas?" the angel guessed, while wondering if any other could compare.

"To a degree," God replied, "to a degree. People go there also to get money that they have not earned."

. . . money that they have not earned.

How tragic that seemed to both angels. . . . people scrambling for money as the supposed key to all their needs!

This other place escaped Darien's attention at first.

"I see New York City, Philadelphia, Father, and Washington, D. C."

"Not there," God said with great patience.

Suddenly Darien knew.

"Atlantic City?" he spoke.

"Yes. . . ."

"How is it different, Father," the angel asked, "that I should minister there instead of Las Vegas?"

"In very important ways."

God paused, thinking of what He had known about Atlantic City over the years, what it was, what it had become, what it served as a symbol of, the pulling of a finger out of a dike that burst and began to flood the nation.

"Gambling was supposed to be the answer to so many urban ills," He spoke. "The tax revenues from it were to be spent for better education, better roads, more policemen, more housing for the poor."

"I see that now, yes, Father, I do."

God was deeply moved by the pathetic sight of men and women at the gambling tables or the slot machines, like starving people at a breadline, holding their breath as they waited for what they thought was all they needed to bring happiness to their lives.

Money.

Pile after pile of money exchanging hands.

"They are blind," God remarked, "lambs who have wandered carelessly away from their shepherd. Grabbing for unholy gains that—"

God lapsed into silence, unable to continue briefly, wrapped up in yet another indication of what human beings were doing to the plan that He had intended for them. He had not failed them, but they had deserted Him anyway.

Darien waited respectfully for a bit, then: "When am I to go, Father? And what am I to do?"

He had been to a host of places at a host of times.

Darien had seen the devastating outbreak of Bubonic Plague in Europe in 1347, as well as the successive epidemics later that century and for several centuries to come. He had stayed with Luther at the start of the Reformation. He experienced the War Between the States. And much more than these, as crucial as such moments were.

And now his mission was to be to Atlantic City. How was it possible to compare what they might accomplish there to what they had seen at other points in history?

Darien thought he knew.

It scarcely matters what destroys someone's life and sends that soul to hell, he told himself. *If war does it, if crime, whatever the cause, if they end up damned forever, then the circumstance should be abhorred, whatever it is.*

God had started to speak again, and Darien listened instantly.

"You cannot change Atlantic City now," God continued, "but you can rescue some of the people. There is one in particular who must be saved because he is so much like others. He is a symbol, Darien."

"What is his name?"

"Bret Erlandson."

A remarkably fine, ethical, wholly decent man, Bret had been the senior class president in high school. He was truly magnetic in his personality. Many of his fellow students thought that he would head into politics or acting or some profession that would put him on display before the public.

Wrong.

All of that speculation was wrong.

He was heading in that direction but he stopped in mid-stride, so to speak. This man named Bret Erlandson stopped because he became convinced that he had been on an ego trip, with his looks and his intelligence giving him a certain power over others, and without his faith to convict him that this would have been very, very destructive to him and those around him. So he left the spotlight, soon got married, and embraced a nondescript but happy and fulfilling lifestyle.

"Does he know Your Son redemptively?" Darien asked.

"He does. And he is a brave man, a relentless one. He is able to get together a group of people and have them unite with him for a common cause, an ability that the gambling interests fear."

"Then his eternal destiny is not at stake."

"It is not, Darien, only the quality of his mortal life is at issue, and what happens to his family. It is important that they do not become discouraged. Bret Erlandson does not know as yet that he will fail in his campaign to keep gambling out of Atlantic City, but even this failure will not stop him from crusading against gambling elsewhere.

"Yet the demonic interests can do little against this man because if he dies from gunshot or knife wound or being run down by a car, the public will rise up in protest. So, they can do little against *him.* He is their greatest enemy, yet they cannot remove him. Instead they must concentrate on other people, defusing his arguments, building up the credibility of their own outlook, and trying to make Bret Erlandson look as though he does not know what he is talking about."

"May I take human form this time, Father? Often, you do not wish that I go so far as that."

"You may."

"When shall I return?"

"You will know, faithful servant, you will know."

And thus it began, the next Angelwalk.

There were other angels in heaven, and many had seen the effects of the gambling syndrome on men, women, and children.

"Worse than alcohol," one angel recalled.

"How can that be?" another asked.

"Alcohol is a part of the gambling addiction. So is cocaine. Gamblers become

depressed over their losses and they need something to pick them up, to keep them going until the next time at the tables or the slot machines. Alcohol and cocaine are crutches for those who have been caught up in the world of gambling."

"It is horrible to learn of this!" the first angel exclaimed.

"More than that," the second added, "it is a tragedy. But then that is what Satan does best: he wraps his poison in a pretty package that is colorful and attractive, and when people swallow it, they find out the truth, that the glittering exterior makes a nightmare that can destroy entire families."

"What he could have been?"

"Lucifer?"

"We knew him so well."

"He was once so fine, so—"

Neither angel could speak of their former comrade any longer.

Quite a contrast existed between an angel like Darien and one like Satan. Both had been inhabitants of heaven long before time and space began.

But Lucifer was the most beautiful of all. Other angels congregated around him, as Darien himself did.

Yet before it was too late, Darien became apprehensive, saw the flowering of ego in Lucifer, saw that his magnificence was not the blessing it should have been but the curse it became, for Lucifer developed jealousy so pervasive, so controlling, so corrosive that it would corrupt him utterly.

Free will.

That was what God had allowed, later, in His human creations, but no less so in His angelic masterworks. They could decide entirely for themselves whom they were to follow.

A third of the angels in heaven clung to Lucifer, fooled by his majesty as they were being enticed by his words.

"Come unto me," he would say to the masses of iridescent creatures, "and I will give you what God has denied."

PROLOGUE

It was power that drew them—power and greed, fueled by ingratitude, encouraged by an angel so special that he seemed to embody Truth nearly as much as did God Himself.

Once they left heaven, they would have many weapons at their disposal: sex, money, and much more—dangled before humankind, all capable of seducing even the best of people, the nicest ones, the most decent.

And gambling was one of these weapons.

Oh, yes, it was. . . .

PART I

They are as sick that surfeit with too much
as they that starve with nothing.

William Shakespeare

It came rather suddenly, this great wave hitting the beachfront of Atlantic City, surging so powerfully that nothing could successfully stand in its way.

Anyone who objected was swept aside or assimilated.

The promises made by gambling interests were extravagant—a cultural and economic rebirth for a town that had been dead for years, only the burial had not as yet been performed. Like a version of the movie queen in Sunset Boulevard, *she was able to trot herself out during the summer, like a grotesque imitation of what she once was. But then when the tourists left just before school started, when the name entertainers decided that there was more money to be made elsewhere, Atlantic City retreated into its shell once again, awaiting next year, when it could emerge from its hibernation—some might say death throes—and pretend that this caricature of health and prosperity during the summer was the real thing, and that there was life in the old girl yet.*

"All of that will be changed," the gambling interests' siren call beckoned. "You will have prosperity year-round, stores and services will be bursting with activity."

A new era.

That was what they said.

CHAPTER 1

Bret Erlandson . . .

In his late twenties, he was tall, blonde-haired, blue-eyed, almost movie-star quality in his looks, a former high school football hero, his hunky build maintained by a regimen of disciplined exercise. He had been rather arrogant during his high school years and never went to college because he felt he did not "need it."

Since his conversion to Christ five years earlier, he had changed considerably. Most of the arrogance was gone but a bit of it did remain, which served him well as he mounted his anti-gambling campaign. His sheer force of will gave him an advantage that eventually was not enough to win the war but helped him bring to each battle a sufficient number of supporters to make the enemy nervous. Make no mistake, this young man was feared by the pro-gambling forces because of his charismatic personality and the sheer determination that he showed day after day.

Bret had been fanatically opposed to any form of gambling in Atlantic City from the beginning of the campaign to get it approved by the proper legislative bodies. In this case, fanaticism was to his credit since it was based upon solid facts and scriptural admonitions that he could not ignore.

"A moral evil," he told ready-to-listen coworkers again and again at the Jersey National Bank, one of the few such institutions that had managed to remain independent. "Can you imagine what will happen to the moral and ethical values of our area when people are drawn to the casinos like bees to honey? We will be overrun with gangsters, whores, real estate speculators—people whose only interest is the pursuit of money, nothing more."

"I know what you mean," replied Sammy Galarza, a fellow teller. "After all, right now times are a little tough, especially during the fall and winter. It's hard on a lot of folks. You can see why gambling would be such a lure to them."

"I agree! During the winter, it's pretty deadly. After the summer season ends in Atlantic City, the whole region goes into hibernation or, better put, a coma."

"Hey, man, did you hear what that commentator said on television the other night?" Bret asked.

"The one about the most desirable and the least desirable cities across the United States?"

"Yeh, that's it. What did you think, bro?"

"I actually did catch it," Sammy acknowledged. "He thinks Vineland, New Jersey, is the armpit of the East."

"I bet he was bought off!" Bret exclaimed, convinced that he had stumbled onto something.

"What do you mean?"

"For not mentioning Atlantic City, that's what I mean. Man oh man, I hate to visualize what part of the human anatomy this guy would think A. C. is if he considers Vineland the armpit!"

Sammy chuckled, since he was rather fond of Vineland, which he found to be a nice country town.

"I have a pretty good idea about that!" he joked.

Sammy became serious for a moment as the two of them sat in the little bank's pleasant lunch room.

"Wouldn't gambling seem to be an answer, then?" he posed, adding quickly, "I'm just theorizing, of course."

"Oh, it is, if you mean plenty of money pouring in, plenty of jobs being created, plenty of media coverage converging on everybody until no one has any peace. Any of these could rejuvenate the entire area."

Bret struggled for an analogy, and then offered a good one.

"It's the way a guy on drugs feels, I guess. He may be depressed but when he snorts some cocaine, he feels better."

"Then he needs more."

"How right you are, Sammy. In time he cannot exist without cocaine, heavier dosages of it, more and more going up his nose until he's rotted away his nasal passages and, soon enough, his brain."

Sammy's face grew pale.

"And then the guy who does this is not only a slave to the drug but also the supplier who makes it available to him."

"Bingo!" Bret told him. "If gambling gets in, you'll have one or two, maybe three, fairly small casinos, then there will be more, and each one will be bigger than the previous casino. Gambling will *dominate* everything. The mob—"

Sammy swallowed hard.

"The mob will control South New Jersey more completely than ever before!" he exclaimed.

"They will own the whole state," Bret pointed out, "because no hard decisions that will negatively impact gambling or *this* part of New Jersey will ever be taken since we will have here a huge percentage of the total taxes collected by Trenton."

"The mob . . ." Sammy repeated. "They've not been fond of Latinos, you know, not for a long time now."

"Why is that?" asked Bret.

"They claim they aren't able to trust us."

"I don't see why."

"It might turn out that we were moles introduced by the Colombians," Sammy told him honestly.

Now Bret could see what his friend was talking about.

"I have read that the Italian mafioso hate the Colombians," he said, "no doubt about that."

Sammy frowned as he asked, "But do you know why?"

Bret shrugged his shoulders.

"Have no idea."

"It's their sense of morality."

Bret pushed himself a few inches away from the table.

"You can't be serious!" he exclaimed. "Gangsters concerned with some point of morality? Unbelievable!"

"Oh, but I am serious, Bret."

"Explain yourself, bro."

"The old-time dons have long hated the idea of drugs," Sammy continued. "It goes against an age-old stricture: you can murder a guy, you can break his legs, or any other part of his body, even scar him for life, but you leave his wife and his kids alone. Drugs hit kids hard, and the dons are uncomfortable with that."

Bret was not prepared to believe all of this.

"You're talking about thugs, gangsters, as though they have some semblance of scruples," he protested. "How can I go along with that?"

Sammy cleared his throat, then added, "It's been that way from the beginning, Bret. Some hot-shot lieutenants have suffered horrible retribution when they miscalculated, and a woman was killed or, worse still, a little girl died as a result of some hit."

He leaned forward on the table.

"On the other hand, those rotten Colombians just don't care what happens to anybody!" he said. "Twenty years from now, an entire nation will tremble at the thought of them, with streets littered with the bodies of anyone opposing them."

As flesh and blood, Sammy could not have guessed how prophetic he would be, but Darien and Stedfast knew all too well since they had the ability to move backward and forward in time and space for a simple reason: time did not exist for either of them. Darien had been in Colombia later, when the drug lords waged war against honest magistrates and others who dared to stand up to them.

"Who is behind the movement for gambling then?" Bret asked.

"The Italians or the Colombians?"

"The Italian mafioso," Sammy replied categorically as he breathed an obvious sigh of relief. "It is almost an answer to prayer."

Sammy knew something that Bret did not. The Colombians had *no* sense of morality or decency. For them, there was no code of ethics. They grew and pushed drugs, and that was the only activity that mattered to them. They had no place for decency.

But, ironically, the Mafia did pay at least lip service to a moral standard *within the family*. And legitimate business deals with outsiders were never handled with less than absolute legality and integrity. To act in any lesser manner was an act of indecency for them.

Bret Erlandson found this extraordinarily hard to believe.

"You can't be serious!" he exclaimed.

"Oh, but I am. There's an expression: 'Better the devil we know than the one we don't.'"

"How is it that you have come to know so much about this sort of thing?" Bret chided his friend.

"I grew up in Brooklyn in a certain neighborhood," Sammy answered, "before the Colombians were even a factor. Some of my friends were real high up in the family that was in power at the time. We used to walk in this one area at midnight."

"Dangerous, I bet."

"You're wrong. Bret. It was the neighborhood that one of the dons absolutely controlled. It's still safer even today than standing in front of the White House in Washington, D.C. at the same hour of the night."

"If gambling wins out in Atlantic City, is that what we'll have then, safe streets?" Bret mused.

That idea intrigued Sammy.

"If a mobster lives in a certain neighborhood, the answer is yes. If a mobster has any *investment* in another, the answer, again, is yes."

He scratched his chin.

"On the other hand, I can't think of any reason why any of the boys, as they are called, would want to move here."

"Better get back to work," Bret said as he glanced at his watch.

Sammy nodded.

"We should talk again," he remarked.

Their lunch break over, both returned to work.

These were men who seemed determined to stand by their convictions. Nothing they could think of seemed able to detour them.

Sammy and Bret were not the only ones. They did not stand alone as they mounted the anti-gambling campaign. Others would join with them. And they would receive support from people of like mind in Las Vegas who provided money to underwrite it.

"We have seen the results morally and spiritually," one after the other would write or telephone, "results glossed over by the huge sums of money pouring in at the state and local levels, but this is all a facade, a facade for an evil that must be stopped in Atlantic City."

CHAPTER 2

Standing by, Darien and Stedfast had been overhearing that conversation, while remaining in their natural invisible states.

"The struggle begins. . . ." Darien observed.

"It cannot be otherwise," agreed Stedfast, his manner melancholy, since he had seen such a struggle firsthand in Las Vegas. "This so-called pastime, this harmless hobby, this foul pursuit of excess coarsens everyone at the same time it applies a coat of sparkling paint, so to speak, to hide what is underneath. I know it too well. I stood in the sands of Las Vegas before a single building had been put up, before the garish neon lights and the laundered money and all the rest that came in."

"You were in the desert, then, with Bugsy Siegel?" Darien asked. "Before Las Vegas was completed?"

"I was, Darien. And the money that man spent brought the wrath of the mob bosses down upon him, of course. After he was murdered, they took over what he started, and ruled unchallenged for decades."

"Has the mob been kicked out?"

"No!" Stedfast exclaimed. "It only *appears* that the gangsters are being left out in the cold. They now own banks, and other financial institutions, and it all seems respectable these days. They finance conglomerates run by their hand-picked men who are the owners of the casinos in Las Vegas and Atlantic City."

"I always thought the Federal authorities were involved as well," Darien questioned, "letting the mob have its way, in return for certain favors."

"I doubt that," Stedfast remarked. "Corrupt judges and bureaucrats and law enforcement officials continue to be 'owned' by the mob, these and other men whom the dons have bought off."

"But, today, not years ago, Stedfast, I am sure the mobsters continue to wield influence in Washington, D.C.; few in that degraded city are beyond their reach."

Darien had good reason to stand by his assertion and made some effort to explain to his comrade why this was so.

"I spent much time in Brooklyn during World War II," he said.

"Tell me about it," Stedfast asked.

"The United States was being overrun by Nazi spies," Darien recalled. "Munitions plants were being blown up, trains carrying weapons derailed, and a great deal else. It seemed that Hitler was losing the war in Europe but winning it in the United States."

"What happened?"

"J. Edgar Hoover, founder and director of the FBI, saw his country potentially collapsing from within."

"And he enlisted the mob to help out?" Stedfast spoke. "That sounds rather bizarre, does it not?"

"Of course, but it was a bizarre time. The U.S. war effort could have collapsed because of the success of more than a hundred Nazi spies and saboteurs. With manpower being concentrated in Europe as well as the Pacific battlegrounds, the Federal authorities did not have the resources they would have preferred to stop this largely successful 'other war' by Hitler's well-trained men and women."

Stedfast had had no idea that the problem of spies and other Nazis infiltrators was so severe.

"Hoover determined that the mobsters were precisely what he needed," Darien continued. "They were tough as well as devious, clever and extraordinarily brutal, not to mention already well-armed, but

Hoover saw to it that they got more munitions: grenades, the most advanced small arms; and so on.

"The Mafia became a second army, and collided with the Nazis many, many times, here and in Italy where Lucky Luciano was responsible almost single-handedly for financing and arming the Italian resistance."

"What happened after the war?"

"Hoover was blackmailed into sticking to his infamous assertion: 'There is no such organization as the Mafia or La Cosa Nostra operating in the United States.' As long as Hoover lived, FBI efforts to bring down the various dons were stunted because, if he did not go along, the media and the government would be given proof about the alliance between the Federal government and the organized criminal underworld."

"So, that is why the gangster element in the United States continues to be so strong?" Stedfast asked.

"Exactly!" Darien agreed. "Because one or more of Hoover's successors still maintain links with the various Mafia families."

"But why? The Second World War ended half a century ago."

"There are other threats."

"The new breed of terrorists?"

"Absolutely, my dear Stedfast. And their kind could be more dangerous than the old-line Nazis because the technology they use is so much more destructive."

Stedfast paused, thinking over a fascinating and unsettling scenario, then broached it to his comrade. "These militia groups, Darien?"

"Yes, those who may have been involved in the Oklahoma City bombing and others around the country?"

"Yes, they *are* a genuine terrorist group."

"Could it be that the Mafia is helping to spot them, and provide leads about the more dangerous groups?"

"Not impossible, I suspect. In fact, you may have hit upon something."

It was Darien's turn to pause, ponder.

"If the Middle Eastern extremists cause more terrorist attacks in the United States, would the Federal authorities tend to use the Mafia to route them out *or* the militia?"

"Or both?"

"I think the Mafia would still be at the center of any such efforts. They have been at this business of subterfuge and violence far longer, in fact, two hundred years."

"Would the dons really want to get involved against the militia groups *and* the terrorists?"

"I think so. Remember, much of the money for both factions comes from aging Nazi industrialists and others who would like to see a Fourth Reich."

"But our mission is about gambling, Darien. Why be concerned about these other matters?"

"Because the Mafia is in all of it, Stedfast. They make a great deal of money from gambling, hundreds of millions of dollars a year."

"Are we here to bring about their downfall then?" his comrade asked, feeling some excitement over the prospect, since every unfallen angel felt the lure of being out there on the spiritual battlefield.

"No, unfortunately," Darien told him, "at least I doubt it."

He, too, felt the pull—he, too, wanted to be battling the great demonic hordes, but that was not to be his station. He accepted the judgment of God, even while harboring some degree of yearning.

CHAPTER 3

Stop the ever-increasing spiral of poverty and despair so rampant in virtually all Native American reservations . . .

Allow gambling on Indian reservations!

Give back to us some shred of dignity.

That was part of the litany some time ago.

If you don't allow gambling, Indian dignity will slide even now.

The white man must not be allowed another cruel blow to the remaining Native American tribes.

Only this wonderful pastime provides the answer.

Darien had been aware of the impact of gambling upon Indians in so many different places.

He knew in advance because he could jump to the future at any point. He was not bound by the rules of time and space.

As it was with Stedfast.

As it was with every other unfallen angel.

But every *fallen* one, Satan and tens of thousands of others, were denied that ability as part of their punishment for rebelling against God.

Native American reservations.

These became a prime target of those greedy men who controlled gambling from Las Vegas but, also, in the backrooms of small restaurants on Mulberry Street in Brooklyn, New York.

Offering a lifestyle that was seldom above either borderline poverty or actually well below that Federal definition, reservations were nothing more than the humiliating final chapter in an embittering saga of once proud Indians whose land was taken from them by expansionist whites over a period of a century.

The gangland bosses, brutish men at best, had succeeded beyond any dreams they might have had. Since 1985, Indian gambling sites had multiplied, with many states allowing them: Washington, Oregon, Idaho, California, Nevada, Arizona, New Mexico, Montana, Wyoming, Colorado, North Dakota, South Dakota, Nebraska, Kansas, Oklahoma, Texas, Minnesota, Iowa, Missouri, Louisiana, Michigan, Mississippi, Alabama, Florida, North Carolina, New York, and Connecticut.

"Liquor and gambling," Darien recalled. "The men go off to the slot machines and the tables while their hapless mates stay home and somehow try to keep their children from turning bad.

"It must be remembered that the various tribes were never as noble as the revisionists would have people believe," Darien spoke, "but, I suppose, in comparison to what they are becoming today—"

Stedfast was amply aware of the unfortunate history of what the other angel was talking about.

"The white world invaded that of the Indians," he recalled, "and then, a hundred-plus years later, came a cruel and yet deceptive death knell: gambling. Whatever values they did have, however pantheistic, were swept away."

Both stopped communicating briefly, transfixed by the duplicity of this monster called gambling. They had just returned from an Indian reservation, having seen one of the most debilitating sights with which they had been confronted on the current journey along Angelwalk—that ancient pathway between heaven and earth along which unfallen angels left and returned to the Creator after accomplishing whatever current mission upon which He in His infinite wisdom had sent them.

A man had lost his paltry savings at the gambling center. To have won big was his last chance. He had only enough money left to buy a bottle of cheap fortified wine. He could not bring himself to go home right away but spent an hour drinking, cursing the Great Spirit and knocking on the doors of people he had thought were his friends but who had become ashamed of him over the months of his slide into alcoholism and drugs and, with virtually equal devastation, gambling.

He had nothing left.

His wife had taken to whoring in nearby Tucson in order to bring in some money, but it was not enough because she was not as attractive as most of the other women of the night, and the johns she got were the ones a little "off," some actually dangerous, men who made her perform acts too perverse for the other whores. Any of her customers could have been a modern Jack the Ripper, but, by chance or providence or whatever, she was saved from being stabbed to death by a stranger.

Her husband had finished the wine.

Knowing his state of mind, knowing how violent his thoughts were, he did try to resist going home right away, and, instead, stumbled into a nearby cemetery, used primarily by the families of Native Americans who had converted to Christianity at whatever point before their deaths.

He shook his fists at the heavens.

"Great Spirit or Jehovah or Jesus or whatever it is that You're supposed to be called! Is this Your idea of revenge? Just because I wouldn't bow down in the dust before You?"

He was feeling emboldened, demonically emboldened.

"I curse You!" he called out. "I—"

Cursing God again, he stumbled toward his trailer, thinking he would find his wife and child inside.

Gone.

But all their clothes remained.

He assumed they had gone outside, perhaps to walk down the road and get a milkshake at Floating Cloud's little stand.

"We can afford that much for our son," he said out loud, then started to sob, "but not much more than that."

So, he decided to wait for them, wait for the beloved members of his family, as he rested a twelve-gauge shotgun on his lap.

"We have a chance," Darien said anxiously.

"So very little time though," mused Stedfast, "we truly cannot let even a second slip by us."

They arrived at the rusty old trailer in an instant, and entered. The man had no idea angels were now with him.

Darien and Stedfast could appear in front of him in human form or they could simply prod his conscience, whispering words of restraint, whatever they could think of in order to stay the hand of self-imposed execution.

Do you really want to do this? Darien spoke but without normal human speech. *They are helpless, innocent.*

The man sat up straight.

"Who's there?" he asked.

They did not answer him.

He slouched back again, gripping the shotgun.

Are you going to blow them to pieces with that? Stedfast said this time. *Wouldn't you give your own life to save theirs if someone else was pointing a shotgun at your wife and your son?*

He dropped the weapon on the floor.

"Am I going crazy?" he shouted. "Just one more stupid—?"

He pressed the palms of his hands against his temple.

What is your name? Darien asked.

"Swift Lightning . . ." the man started to say, "my Indian name. The one I use on my income tax is—"

He stopped himself, looking around the confines of the cramped trailer.

Swift Lightning, you mustn't take your own life, and the lives of your loved ones! Darien went on. *You can help one another. They can be at your side until you are able to get your life back together.*

He reached for the shotgun, and held it menacingly.

"Whoever you are," Swift Lightning said, "you're ignorant. My wife's become a whore. And they're both going to leave me. What will I have left then, anyway?"

He shut out the voices, aided by those demonic forces that had managed to gain control of him.

Both Darien and Stedfast realized that they could do nothing.

"We cannot force our way in," Darien observed. "Nor can Satan for that matter. We have to come in through the Holy Spirit by invitation, as demons have to do through Satan by invitation."

Nor could they continue to "talk" to him. A barrier as impenetrable as though it were concrete was up now.

All both angels were able to do was stay, and wait, and hope for an opening, a moment when—

"I am so weary," Stedfast said. "Whether it's gambling or pornography or something else, you and I must deal with the addictive behavior of men and women every moment that we spend on Planet Earth.

"The danger about gambling is that it looks so good. Someone can indulge it in the midst of a colorful environment, with laughter in the background, and beautiful lights, and people often dressed in expensive clothes walking floors covered with plush carpeting or expensive tiles.

"There is an air of excitement, thrills, the potential of instant wealth. Everything is calculated to aid the mood the casino entrepreneurs are trying to create—an environment free of restraint, and one that seems wholly isolated from the real world."

Darien agreed, and added, "Whereas pornography is, by its nature, an addiction that does not flourish in the midst of a carnival-like atmosphere. It is one pursued in true solitary confinement.

"It invades the privacy of a man and a woman and puts their most personal behavior on display, not at the center of bright lights and nearby laughter but flickering images on a viewer that costs a quarter of a dollar to operate for a minute or two, then another quarter, on and on, dollars spent.

"The addict leaves that little booth with its peep-hole enticements, and walks past aisles of so-called marital aids, XXX-rated videos, and more. He buys a twenty-dollar video that cost a dollar to make, plus some magazines with erotic contents, and he is on his way home, to the privacy of a room, shutting out everything but what he has purchased, which will keep him going for the rest of the evening until he falls asleep, and his dreams, springing from his degraded imagination, provide more sick and defiling stimulation."

Both angels were saddened.

They had been with God at the birth of a planet once conceived as the centerpiece of His creation. They had experienced Eden. They had known of what their Creator intended for the human race since before time began.

"I want a world of endless beauty," God had said. "I want a world where nothing has to die that other life might live. I want a world that those in heaven can visit openly, and converse with their flesh-and-blood relatives."

Relatives . . .

That was God's intention, for angels and humans alike to be living in sublime peace side by side.

"Oh my . . ." Darien said as he recalled what had been started, first with Adam and Eve, with the intention of spreading their seed throughout the earth.

"Remembering?" Stedfast asked of his comrade.

"Yes, dear friend, I am remembering. . . ."

"If only . . ."

"No use, Stedfast."

"I know, but it is so difficult not to think back and see the beginning so sublime as it was. . . ."

One by one, Satan gained victories—first, with Adam and Eve, then with their son Cain and, later, with King David and a vast number of other men and women from ancient Israel on to the period of the widespread persecution of devout Christians by Roman emperors and beyond that.

CHAPTER 3

"So many lives lost, Stedfast," Darien moaned, "blood-soaking soil that was meant to be pure."

They were deeply affected by the magnitude of barbaric behavior that they had witnessed, including the Inquisition and the Crusades.

"The Inquisition was purely Satanic," Darien spoke, "but it was the Crusades that proved the most frustrating."

"Frustrating?" Stedfast repeated, puzzled.

"Oh, yes."

"In what way?"

"They started out not as they became. Europe was being threatened with a massive Muslim invasion. So, the Crusades were essentially defense-by-offense. Preventing Europe from being overrun, the Crusaders invaded Muslim territory."

"What went wrong?"

"Even the best of men are susceptible to becoming corrupt in part or in totality. Ultimately, their egos bloated by the initial victories, and the Crusades fell victim to bloodlust. They got away from merely beating back and defeating the enemy to an obsession with annihilating the heathens.

"Women and children were slaughtered, whole villages completely demolished. The Muslims fought back with renewed fury, and bodies from both sides were piled high on the various battlefields."

That grisly vision made them both stop and analyze a question that they were forced to confront: With so much killing in the twentieth century, whether in war or a drive-by shooting or a madman entering a schoolyard and mowing down helpless children or slaughtered by tyrannical rulers, was gambling so bad by contrast?

Why bother with it?

They could be off to a barrio, for example, trying to bring sanity to neighborhoods torn apart by drug-dealing, drive-by shootings, and other forms of social decay.

Or genocide-torn Bosnia.

Or far too many other places where atrocities were happening.

After all, gambling provided a means of entertainment and relaxation.

Not all players lost. Quite a number won.

And look at the employment that was provided.

Yes, the angels knew, all of that was true, but gambling's continued success rested on a foundation that no Christian could accept: acceptance of a corrupt pastime and *growing* numbers of gamblers, a percentage of which would become addicts.

Addiction . . .

For these individuals, gambling was to be an obsession, taking control of their lives. But then that really was what it all amounted to, a glittering face on an old problem.

As with cigarettes . . . as with drugs . . . as with sex. . . .

People unable to stop.

But society said that that was okay. It did not matter that a *few* lives were ruined as long as *many* lives were helped.

As they waited in Swift Lightning's trailer, neither angel could come up with an answer as to why they were there and not in Spanish Harlem or other places around the country where violence occurred daily and death could intrude in an instant from the open window of a souped-up muscle car.

Until Swift Lightning's family arrived.

In one quick movement, as his wife opened the door, he pulled the trigger of that shotgun and killed them both, then he got a pistol from a nearby cabinet, put the barrel in his mouth, and—

The two angels could do nothing but watch—which is what had happened to them often over the centuries, watching as Christians were attacked by wild beasts while large Roman crowds cheered, watching as men, women, and children were crucified, watching as the march of history showed the imprint of Satan.

Sometimes there were successes for Darien and Stedfast. Sometimes they prevented suicide, murder, and acts of perversion.

"We have to remember those," Stedfast spoke as they looked at what was left of Swift Lightning's head. "We have to—"

CHAPTER 3

He turned away, leaving that trailer only to be confronted with the unholy mess strewn outside.

Darien joined his comrade.

"What good are we?" Stedfast lamented frankly. "Three human beings dead, just look at them, including an innocent child. And all the while, more families are being ruined by damned gambling."

That was not a profanity from an unfallen angel incapable of it.

It was a statement.

Nothing more.

For gambling, without question, was damned by God—damned because of what it caused, opening the floodgates to a variety of other sins such as prostitution, drug addiction, and alcoholism.

Yet not only that . . .

Damned for what it was—an enticement to love money.

Gambling caused money to be viewed as something that should be coveted, like blood in the veins, like oxygen in the lungs, pursued fanatically in the midst of a phony, revved-up environment that, in Las Vegas and Atlantic City, was controlled by self-deceived men principally from Italy. It imposed upon the Italian people a blight that they had never been able to live down, crass men who made their profits from the addictions of others, addictions that went beyond gambling itself—prostitution and alcoholism and drugs—all fostered by the glittering facade of the casinos, behind which cheap women flaunted their physical attributes sheathed in expensive gowns, whispering the calls of Homeric sirens.

And the good people of Las Vegas and Atlantic City, the decent men and women, the Christians and others appalled by all that gambling stood for, but who had to live somewhere—they could only protest, but not very effectively, because gambling's influence had become part of virtually every aspect of life. Many churches accepted money from the gambling interests; many rehabilitative charities depended on similar donations; state and local tax revenues were interwoven with the large sums that gambling generated; and all the rest of it. Meanwhile, an unstoppable cancer continued to spread.

Darien was no less affected by Stedfast but his missions—past and present—along Angelwalk had been more far-reaching. He once was committed, during an earlier period, to finding the reality of Satan in the world because at that time he was not quite certain that his former comrade's treatment was entirely justified. What he uncovered proved that Satan was being treated by God precisely as he should have been.

Since then, with his doubts settled, Darien was being assigned very much as a comforter, aiding the Holy Spirit but, also, going off by himself and helping men, women, and children whenever possible.

There had been striking successes—for one, the conversion of a mass murderer just weeks before his scheduled execution—but these were exceptions.

"I suppose we should go to Atlantic City now," Stedfast spoke, eager to see anything else that gambling had wrought.

"I would have thought that, yes," Darien replied.

Stedfast knew every mood, every nuance of the other angel's personality, and so he asked, "But God is telling you something else?"

Darien was hardly surprised, after the two having spent eons together, that Stedfast had guessed so correctly.

"He is."

Stedfast was suddenly hopeful, hopeful that God was sending them on another mission altogether.

"Are we to abandon any work in Atlantic City?" he asked, the expectancy he felt apparent.

"No," Darien replied, "we are instead to stop in Las Vegas before we go on to New Jersey."

"Why does God want us to do this?"

"I cannot say."

Stedfast was not, in any way, a rebellious angel, so resigning himself to the situation at hand was not difficult for him.

"We can only obey in faith," he said.

"As ever, Stedfast, as ever."

CHAPTER 4

What of the action-adventure movie star who did a televised appeal for the legality of gambling not to be overturned on Indian reservations?

His image was famous to millions of fans. In recent years his popularity had enjoyed a shot in the arm by the highly rated TV series which he produced and in which he starred on a weekly basis.

There could be no doubt about his sincerity. Or his honesty.

Undoubtedly this man, a decent, honorable chap, *was wholly* sincere, a sincerity underlined by the fact that he was part-Indian himself.

However, he had obviously bought into the conventional wisdom that gambling was okay, so long as its proceeds were of benefit to Native Americans. In other words, people could sin so long as they got something out of it.

To make sure that non-Native American viewers felt threatened, a warning was flashed on the screen that twelve thousand WASP jobs were in jeopardy if gambling were taken away from the reservations.

Propaganda . . .

Of the rankest sort.

And it was apparently approved by a movie star who had increasingly declared his concern for family values.

"How can he do this?" Stedfast asked. "How can he support a so-called pastime that is morally corrupting and, often, financially destructive?"

Neither angel ascribed questionable motives to the man. He was known as a straight arrow, and had even cooperated with some Christian groups that were hoping he could give at least one episode of his TV series each season a "redemptive" dimension. He was sympathetic, pledged to do so, and came through as he had agreed, pleasing millions of Christian fans.

And yet—

. . . a so-called pastime that is morally corrupting and, often, financially destructive.

"He can do this because some people *do* benefit from the suffering of others," Darien spoke. "He must be deluded into thinking that this is acceptable if it means those who are hit hard are not Native Americans. You have to admire the man's uncompromising loyalty to his people."

"Does he not know that much of the profit from Indian casinos goes to outsiders, not Native Americans themselves?" Stedfast added.

"A new exploitation by white men!"

"No doubt about that, Darien, no doubt at all. In fact, some tribes have been struggling to pay off debt and management fees imposed by white entrepreneurs. Where is the emancipation in that?"

"Another lie," Darien agreed, "another deception fostered by longtime masters of duplicity. After all, the various Mafia families have been deceiving themselves since soon after the birth of Cosa Nostra two hundred years ago in Sicily."

"If they did not do this, if they did not believe the lie, they would not be able to live with their consciences as they looked back over a field of murdered human beings piled up as a result of their violent excesses.

"Gambling is just another kind of gun held to the heads of men and women who have been roped in like the victims ensnared on a poisonous spider's web."

Time to leave . . .

With regret and an encompassing melancholy, the two angels finally left the Indian reservation casinos, left the sight of people driving themselves like lemmings over a cliff even as they were deceived into thinking that instead they were on the verge of personal and racial rebirth long overdue.

Darien and Stedfast headed toward Las Vegas, on their way to Atlantic City.

Even as they did, they noticed a so-called public service plea on a television in the window of a store. It featured a leading action-adventure star pleading with people to stop the move to make casinos on reservations illegal.

"But why?" Darien asked. "Why exhort the uncomprehending to stand in the way of righteousness? The Indian thirst for gambling revenues is but one more indication of the spiritually lost nature of people who are largely without Christ.

"They already wallow in naked pantheism. Their rate of alcoholism is higher than the national average. Their value system is completely ashambles. Why add yet another avenue of deterioration?"

Stedfast agreed without hesitation. This angel had been present with the Navajos and others during the last century as various denominations saw in them a potentially dynamic harvest of lost souls. While the resulting missionary outreach was often heavy-handed, that alone was not what doomed the spirited attempts to bring various tribes into the body of Christ.

Indians had been married to idol worship and demonic enslavement for many, many generations, and their hearts had hardened, in most cases, for time and eternity—this process aided by the acknowledged cruelty of white soldiers who treated them with contempt and appalling acts of inhumanity, including raiding villages and sticking babies on the tips of bayonets, bragging in letters written to loved ones at home about their triumphs in the war against the savages, and mentioning nothing about the loss of their humanity as acts of sheer barbarism increased.

These kinds of atrocities were the white man's infamy, but then, in supporting gambling, Indian leaders seemed needlessly bent on their own destruction in the same way that Las Vegas and Atlantic City had been eroding the moral and spiritual fiber of those caught up in gambling's web.

"So dangerous . . ." Darien spoke.

"The brainwashing?" asked Stedfast.

"Yes, that. If you vote against gambling on Indian reservations, you are not only being a bigot but you are callous and unfeeling toward the poor."

"Clever as always."

"Satan was never deemed stupid. He is, in effect, considerably smarter than many of the righteous.

"Indians think that white men owe them this way out of their plight."

Darien paused, saddened.

"I will be so very glad when Satan is finally punished, when he can no longer deceive anyone."

Stedfast felt as his comrade did. As angels devoted to the God of truth, they were sickened by duplicity.

"What happens when truth hits the Indians involved in gambling? The truth that white men benefit enormously, especially certain big corporations, and that the Indians are only pawns in this scheme for ever greater profits?"

Darien could envision the possibilities.

"Greater despair among the tribes," he offered.

"Despair can lead to bloodshed."

"It can, Stedfast, it surely can."

PART II

Corruption is like a ball of snow:
whence once set a-rolling it must increase.

Charles Caleb Colton

Lies.

So many lies.

Satan was the father of these, and of every other form of corruption.

That fact was not new to Darien, but one with which he had been familiar for centuries by measuring, and before time was ever concocted.

The reason he began his Angelwalk series of odysseys was to trace both the origin and the continuance of corruption, not because of any kinds of doubts that it did exist but, rather, concern over how pervasive, and, most importantly, how much actually could be traced to Satan himself.

At one time Darien actually did wonder if his former comrade Lucifer could be responsible for all of the crime, perversity, evil that ever existed over the long history of the Human Race.

What he discovered, as he swept through the millennia of time and space, was that Satan truly was the originator of corruption, bringing it first to the garden of Eden—again in itself not a startling new fact as far as he was concerned, but after that, determined to corrupt everything else that God had created, including the family unit, and the church.

But not every act was of his doing.

Once corrupted, human nature continually proved very much able, on its own, to covet, to lie, to steal, to rape, to murder, to lust, to pervert—a familiar list of sins that demons always encouraged.

And then, as these had taken hold, the demons stepped aside. Human beings, having succumbed, blindly furthered the devil's designs.

Gambling was a demonic favorite.

This was the case because it was one sin that brought many others with it, including alcoholism, drug addiction, and prostitution.

And it was spawned from the love of money, and greed was a progeny.

Gambling could not be sold even to the most gullible unless it was "packaged" prettily, and that it was.

But there had to be a way to reach whole families, not just a few select individuals. There had to be a way of making gambling seem harmless.

And so a new emphasis began in Las Vegas.

Las Vegas, yes . . .

Home of prostitution, suicide, larceny, and a variety of other crimes, a town spawning violence, greed, and much more.

No more that.

A makeover was in progress.

Las Vegas . . . the family resort town.

Bring the kids and have fun!

Would every youngster go on to be a gambler? Of course not!

But many would. And that was the point: Expose them to gambling now, and, the gambling power brokers gloated, we will get them later when they have money of their own to spend.

How demons rejoiced!

CHAPTER 5

The two angels were anxious to begin their mission in Atlantic City—anxious to do what they could, save lives, stymie the work of the legions of demons that they knew were at work in and around the casinos.

"Whenever there is gambling," Darien spoke, "there is demonic activity."

Stedfast could not disagree with that.

"I think you are right," he said. "To see the bright lights, to hear the music, to look at the stage shows, you would think entertainment."

Darien nodded, his form shimmering with anger.

"So deceptive," he added. "Satan thinks most people are fools."

"Those who become entrapped by gambling *are* fools."

"Yet if anyone who is of flesh and blood speaks out against this so-called pastime, he is labeled right-winger."

Despite the solemnity, Stedfast suddenly started laughing.

"My right wing has never given me difficulty in flight," he said. "It's the left that has been troublesome."

Darien was not amused, and Stedfast apologized for his lame attempt at humor.

God had assigned them to visit a Native American reservation in the western United States, and, second, on to Las Vegas *before* eventually ending up in that century-old seaside resort.

And, truly, they were in the dark as to the reason. But then that was not unusual even as they simply surrendered to God, and did what He asked of them. Anything else would have meant the two angels taking the same path as Lucifer traveled eons ago.

"We question sometimes," Darien pondered briefly. "Is that wrong? I wonder. . . ."

"So do I," remarked Stedfast.

"Should we be ashamed?"

"Of questions?"

"Yes, of questions."

Stedfast was not usually the one who dealt with such questions. But he was grateful for the opportunity.

"We have the same free will that humankind has," he spoke with some solemnity.

"I know," Darien said, a bit annoyed that his comrade had stated something so obvious. "And yet—"

"Why does this bother you?" asked Stedfast.

"Human beings are riddled with questions." Darien spoke with an unintentional hint of contempt.

"So should we be any different, my comrade Darien?" suggested Stedfast. "We are creations of God as they are."

"Not quite."

"What do you mean?"

"We are not quite the same as they."

"Yes, I know," Stedfast agreed, "for they are flesh and blood and not spirit—not yet anyway."

"We are different otherwise."

"How?"

"We were created first. We were born in the mind of God before anything else was conceived."

Stedfast did not have to be reminded of that, but he was glad that Darien had done so. Memories were stirred—memories that could not, should not, be forgotten, for they were antidote to the depression that demons threatened to foist even upon them.

"Oh, Darien, back then . . ."

"So glorious . . . nothing but what seemed the eternality of joy, pure joy, unending, or so we thought."

"We were nurtured in the mind of God," Stedfast added. "That was our womb. Oh, Darien, I miss it so much!"

It was not a truth unknown to these two angels but a truth that never ceased to cause a wave of awe to overwhelm both.

"The clarity!" Darien exclaimed. "We saw everything through His vision, His perfectness. We could look from one galaxy to another and find only richness, not a single destroyed planet, no barren continents and dried-up river beds. No pollution, no sin, no pain or suffering anywhere."

The length and the breadth and the depth of all that was, even the tiniest aspect of creation, shared the glory of God because *everything* extended from Him, a unity that seemed, subsequently, inconceivable, obscured by the division that followed the cataclysm known as the Casting Out.

"It seemed as though the galaxies were a part of their Creator, no separation of any kind. His radiance, His goodness, His honor and joy, and all else about Him were the center of what they were."

Darien was often drawn back to that scene but then he had to return to present reality, and it chilled him.

"Look at everything out there!" he said, looking up at the stars. "Death from one inconceivably distant end to the other. The moon barren. Mars as well. Jupiter nothing but flames and gasses."

Stedfast was feeling the other angel's melancholy.

"I think . . ." he began, then hesitated.

"Yes, my friend?" Darien asked.

"I think gambling is a modern forbidden fruit."

"What made you think of that?"

"Satan's rebellion, the death and decay we now see on other planets, no life anywhere. Satan has been trying to make Earth just like the rest."

"Driving out beauty and purity, and decency and—"

Darien shook himself, becoming as depressed and as given to righteous anger as was Stedfast.

"With the fruit of the tree of the knowledge of good and evil," Darien mused, "Satan was seemingly offering something so simple to Adam and Eve. What could possibly be wrong? Despite God's admonition against tasting of it, He would *never* become too mad at His precious creations."

"Exactly. That is what Satan must have been thinking, that is what he told Adam and Eve in so many words. That is what he is telling people about gambling. And they are seduced by the tens of thousands until there is nothing left—so many families devastated by financial loss, wracked by arguments, some turning to violence. And yet it all began with an insinuating temptation: 'Try the crap tables. See what you can do at the one-armed bandits. Just a quarter or a dollar or two. What could be the harm of it?'

"Our former comrade has never changed," Stedfast moaned.

Darien recalled rather wistfully what Lucifer, later Satan, was like in heaven before the Casting Out.

You were so brilliant, he thought, *so stunning to look at. You outshone the rest of us, and yet we did not feel jealous. We just accepted what you were, the highest expression of God's creative impulse, the greatest being in all of eternity, apart from the heavenly Father Himself. So many angels flocked around you, listening to your apparent wisdom, captivated by your personality.*

Darien had seen Satan since then, no hint of his former beauty left. That which had fueled his arrogance ironically now did not exist. And he would be forever condemned to knowing that it would never be his again, no matter how hard he fought against the One who had given him life.

You use any scheme to destroy those who have accepted Christ into their lives as well as those who have not before they change their minds, he told himself. *You are unable to admit that it is over. All that is left are the death throes of your rebellion.*

With Satan, gambling had honed the art of deception that he practiced to an extraordinary degree. As Darien and Stedfast entered one of the Las Vegas casinos, they knew what he was up to instantly.

The glitter . . .

"You would think that he could not outsmart anyone with this," Stedfast observed. "If I were human—even though subject to their sin nature, which tends to blind them, and blind them badly—the very falseness of this place, the cold opportunism of it, would be more than enough to alert me."

The neon lights, the piped-in music, the deliberate emphasis upon a collision of every conceivable color, the freely flowing alcohol, the buxom women and their little purses, which had become the symbol of the modern-day whore. . . .

"There is something else," Darien pointed out. "The heartlessness, Stedfast, the utter lack of compassion."

. . . the utter lack of compassion.

That had been at the center of Las Vegas since the beginning. The casinos beckoned, "Come in, and let us destroy you."

"Look at that one," Stedfast said, pointing to a tall, broad-shouldered, silver-haired man in his late forties who moved confidently among the whores and the bouncers as well as patrons with diamonds and furs and imported Italian shoes, comfortable among them. "We have seen him before, you know, but he was dressed differently, wearing leather cowboy clothes, and with two days' growth of beard on his face."

Vincenzo "Vinnie the Bear" DiCosolo.

The essence of Las Vegas, smiling, well-groomed, outwardly "user-friendly," but in league with the forces of darkness, he had taken the mantle of Bugsy Siegel, Howard Hughes, Sam Giancanna, and others and had given it his own twist, one that could be summed up in a single word: charm.

Over the years, Vinnie the Bear had been close to President Lyndon Baines Johnson and other influential individuals in Washington, D.C. He had provided some of the women President John Fitzgerald Kennedy saw during his years in the White House. But, knowing him for what he was, Gerald Ford, Jimmy Carter, Ronald Reagan, and George Bush would have nothing to do with him.

During the dry years, he could do little more than expand his already enormous influence throughout Nevada.

And this he pursued almost maniacally.

Whether bribing officials on the one hand or sponsoring media-savvy charities on the other, he was a dazzling success—his exposure on the various media well-calculated and persistent. Every few weeks, something "new" was covered, the "script" written and approved by Vinnie himself.

Vinnie existed for this sort of thing.

He needed the recognition.

Unlike John Gotti, though, he never alienated the mob bosses; he delighted them. Gotti drew attention to the mafioso, but Vinnie diverted it to the aura of respectability that he helped the eager mobsters to construct—to their facade, yes, but not to *them,* which was what brought Gotti down.

He could convince or threaten or bribe anyone, it seemed, to sacrifice their ethics, their morality, every vestige of decency that they had, if not in one sudden turnabout, then in nearly imperceptible incremental stages—often so subtly that only hindsight, years later, gave them any clue as to what had happened.

He did it to the Indians.

And he did it brilliantly.

He came across to them initially as a white man with conscience.

"Wounded Knee was what opened my eyes," he said early on as he met with one of the Native American governing councils. "And there have been so many other tragedies foisted upon you by the Federal government."

His eyes filled with tears on cue.

"I am ashamed of the color of my skin," he sobbed, "because of what it has come to mean, what it *says* to you and your brothers."

With absolute sincerity, he told them that if he could renounce his birthright as a white man, he would do that.

"But since that is impossible," he stressed, "let me do something that I hope will convince you that I have a conscience, and that I want to renounce the acts that have been perpetrated against you."

He presented a plan. And gambling was the nucleus of it.

"This cannot happen immediately," he said. "It will take years, I can tell you that. But then you have waited many decades for justice, and justice will *never* be yours, I am afraid. That time has passed."

He was playing them well, having studied what made them tick.

"But you can reclaim some of what the Feds ripped from your grasp," he added. "You can say good-bye to the poverty and claim prosperity instead."

They were interested, their body language making their unspoken reactions embarrassingly transparent.

"With the money, you can buy land—land out here in the West, and land elsewhere. You can invade New England with money, and take over business after business. You can guarantee that your children will never go hungry again."

And so it went.

Casinos on Indian land became a reality, enraging the white establishment and delighting all those Native Americans who dreamed of striking back.

"This is Little Big Horn all over again, without all the blood and guts," one leader told Vinnie. "They lost this time around as well, they lost big-time, and there's very little that any of them can do to stop us."

Vinnie smiled maliciously.

"We can buy *their* land right out from under them," the leader said, licking his lips in an uncharacteristic show of emotion. "The Japanese are doing it. So are the Iranians. Why not us? We were here before any of them!"

"It's the way I planned things, my friend," Vinnie replied. "Hey, I'm good at this, and you know it."

"We owe you a debt," the leader assured him. "Whatever you need, ask."

If some official needed "convincing," that could be arranged.

Normally, Vinnie DiCosolo could make just one call to Brooklyn for that sort of thing, but the more his mafiosi cohorts seemed uninvolved, to the outside world, the better they liked it, stepping in only if an emergency were to arise.

Indians were again being manipulated and victimized by the white man, but in a way that they could not have anticipated.

CHAPTER 6

Las Vegas . . .

It was a center of everything that was abhorrent to the two angels who found it the final stop on their way to Atlantic City. But this was a different Las Vegas than the one they had expected. The bright lights were present; the long black or white limos dispensing fat cats with cigars and women with often greatly exaggerated bosoms that virtually none made any effort to hide; the fanatical expressions on the faces of those who were determined to make money from one-armed bandits; the hidden cameras, the lurking bouncers, the side rooms where drugs were handed out free to favored customers; and more that was slimy and evil and ultimately degrading.

. . . a different Las Vegas than the one they had expected.

A new emphasis had taken over, fostered by one man: Vincenzo DiCosolo. It was as though everything led to him—this hulking, supposedly sophisticated embodiment of all that gambling was and wanted to be.

Family town . . .

A wonderful place where families could spend their time—the adults off to the casinos, the children to their kiddieland thrills and knights-in-shining-armor attractions, the new and superficially pleasant facade for evil. How familiar a ring that had to Darien and

Stedfast, the sugar coating of sin, making it seem more palatable, even harmless.

Something of that was what Vinnie DiCosolo had envisioned a long time before, shifting the focus to save the town.

And he had a good reason.

A visionary, he seemed to have a kind of crystal-ball ability implanted in his brain—senses that allowed him to extrapolate that which would escape other men.

Demonically inspired . . .

What else could it be, taking a practice, a lifestyle that God loathed, that was an insult to His holy nature, and putting it on a spotlighted pedestal, advertising it, promoting it, changing it from something loathsome into a magnet for the unwary.

Oh, yes, it was demonically inspired, and this cohort of demonic entities used it to the hilt, not knowing or wanting to know the identity of the master puppeteer who was pulling his strings.

One day, he was standing in front of a casino.

A blackout had occurred because that summer was especially hot, and air conditioning demands outpaced the ability of the utility company to provide current.

So, everything shut down.

Las Vegas, in an instant, grounded to a halt, tens of millions of dollars of business evaporating.

Someone else might have seen God's judgment as the cause, but Vinnie the Bear looked at it another way.

This is what will happen to Las Vegas as times change during the next twenty years, he thought. *We need to change with them. Disneyland and Disney World and Universal Studios are successful because—*

He snapped his fingers as the concept burgeoned.

The idea of gambling *per se* would be gradually soft-pedaled, with another emphasis taking its place.

Las Vegas as a family resort. . . .

A concept brilliant in its simplicity!

CHAPTER 6

But as smart as Vincent DiCosolo was, he had never been allowed absolute autonomy by his underworld cronies before then. He had to call the heads of the various crime families together and present to them what it was that he had in mind.

Just getting "the lads" together at a considerable distance from Brooklyn, Chicago, and Miami, with only the Los Angeles crowd getting off easy, required planning that was far from casual.

Though the mafioso had known "peace" between the families for longer than usual, total trust was still missing.

No one wanted to be led into a trap.

Ambushes seemed to belong to other, more violent eras, but then who could be sure? Nobody was willing to travel anywhere unless the tightest security measures were applied, tighter than any accorded the president of the United States.

A month later, the biggest assembly of mafioso kingpins in years met in a large conference room at one of Las Vegas' top hotels.

"Vegas has been a place which only adults have felt that they can visit," he told the men, who seemed right out of central casting in terms of being Mafia types. "We have been called 'Sin City' by some of the church groups. We have to change that, at least enough so that the public relations people have something to work with."

Everyone present was studying him intently, men who did not have the word *gullible* in their personal vocabulary, and who would have reacted violently if they smelled a pitch that was a con game designed to bilk them out of their dirty money.

"Eventually one generation will die out," Vinnie continued, "and if we don't reach the one after it, this town will die."

None of the visitors said anything initially.

Most just puffed on their cigars or their pipes as they waited for Vinnie the Bear to finish his spiel.

"How do we go about achieving this?" he asked, while having the answers close to his lips so that he could tell them right away.

He waited, looking from don to don, knowing that each one

needed to be convinced beyond any doubt, or he risked Bugsy's fate.

"We get them to bring the kids," he went on, "and we get the kids to like what they see and hear."

One of the men stood up abruptly.

"And they return when they're grown-up to spend big bucks!" he declared as he smiled broadly.

"Precisely my point!" Vinnie agreed. "We can't lose. The hotel revenues go up, the dinner tabs and, above all, the income from the casinos themselves. Only one area will not show an increase."

Their expressions showed that they were puzzled.

"The whores," he told them. "Nothing we can do about that."

General laughter.

"So there it is," Vinnie said. "What do you think?"

Though he had had to become unerringly adept at hiding his genuine emotions, he was still a bit concerned that the dons would see how nervous he was. After all, he was banking a great deal on their acceptance of what he offered because rejection of the plan would have been a blow to his credibility and would limit his options if any other ideas occurred to him down the pike.

Finally . . .

There was general agreement that he had hit upon a win-win formula, and, therefore, he was given a blank check.

"Do what it takes," said a five-foot-tall but exceedingly powerful man named Rocco from a certain neighborhood in Brooklyn, N.Y. "You spend every dollar you have to, and then figure in a bonus for yourself."

Vinnie the Bear was given a triumphant standing ovation.

Las Vegas the family resort was born. . . .

When the two angels learned of the attempt to bring in children, they wanted to skip Las Vegas. The idea of getting young ones exposed to the atmosphere of a gambling town, opening up the door for later obsession with the pastime, left no doubt about who was pulling Vinnie's strings.

CHAPTER 6

Or was it something deeper, even more sinister?

Stedfast gave that notion some thought.

"Is he a demon in human flesh?" he ruminated. "If he is, do we know the fallen comrade from heaven?"

"I wonder . . ." Darien replied. "I wonder about the likelihood of that, as you do. Let me ponder this matter for a bit."

Darien took the other angel's question and seriously considered it.

If it worked out that they could be with DiCosolo alone, one or both of them could then try to talk to the indwelling presence. They had done this sort of thing countless times over the course of human history. If no response came forth, then Vinnie the Bear was controlled by Satan but without one of damnation's henchmen *inside* him.

"I doubt it, my comrade," Darien told him. "Demons have never been under every rock, you know."

"Of course not. I was just wondering if this DiCosolo is an exception. He does appear so slick, so smooth, so convincing that he seems to be imbued with special abilities beyond most men."

"He is sold out, but he is not possessed. Satan does not waste his troops when they are not really needed."

Stedfast could agree with that.

He had witnessed the results of the devil's wiles for many centuries and had come to understand that human nature was capable of corrupt actions all by itself, allowing Satan to keep his "troops" for other situations, such as fomenting civil wars, planning race riots, aiding the rise of infanticide in one form or another.

"Look at this man," Stedfast said as they watched Vinnie being picked up by a limo and hurried out of town toward the Las Vegas airport. "He is obviously intelligent, and he has a charming personality. He seems to be the sort of individual whom certain kinds of people instinctively trust, and yet he is working for the forces of hell."

"And trying to get others to follow almost in virtual lockstep behind him," Darien added. "Mothers and fathers are having their lives devastated by the financial and emotional burdens that gambling heaps upon them, and then their children years later continue down the same awful path."

It was not an unfamiliar tale, a new plot devised by a master storyteller but something quite old. The miracle of it was how people kept falling for the same deception—the disguising of evil to make it seem not a repulsive force from hell, not something that could never give birth to the good, the decent, the uplifting—but a foul influence, this evil, reeking with perversity, taking the innocent and turning it into the pathetic, a shell of what once was, and never would be again.

CHAPTER 7

Just twenty years would have to pass before Vinnie the Bear's dream came into full fruition.

And the "wisdom" of it would be heightened by the competition that Atlantic City would eventually give to Las Vegas, offering an alternative that, for people in the heavily populated area east of the Mississippi, would be far more convenient since Atlantic City is only a relatively short bus ride away.

Vinnie knew all about "the queen of resorts," as the town had been called for most of the twentieth century, often sarcastically. For a very long time, he had studied everything he could about it, compiling his own set of demographics. And he quickly suspected what would happen as gambling in Atlantic City gained momentum.

So, he positioned Las Vegas differently.

Gone were the necessity and the uncertainty engendered by checking everything through with the mob bosses first. He could get a hundred million dollars "overnight" if he really needed to do so, with a minimum of explanations.

Success.

That was what these men of darkness respected, and that was what Vincenzo DiCosolo gave them.

And he proved to be extraordinarily good at it.

Darien and Stedfast knew this because they had a singular ability, the same one that Darien alone had used during his original Angelwalk. They traveled ahead by two decades and saw what Vinnie would do then, and, subsequently, they returned to Las Vegas while the upgrading of Atlantic City was yet in its infancy.

Neither angel was bound by time.

What they were accustomed to was eternity itself, where time could be only a meaningless concept, a simple contrivance for the use of finite minds incapable of coping with anything else.

Human beings were like sheep.

Tyrants such as Hitler and Stalin and the other evil men of human history would speak of them in this manner with nothing but contempt, spitting on the ground afterwards as though clearing their mouths of a bitter taste.

But Jesus spoke of sheep with love, those sheep that were His holy responsibility—men, women, and children to care for, to guide along the rocky paths ahead of them, making sure that they did not lose their way as they were drawn to their ultimate destination.

Heaven . . .

Where there were no days or weeks or months or years, not even decades or centuries, nor any need for these.

Eternity was, rather, a seamless succession of events and relationships unhampered by mortality, of wonder and beauty that did not end, of health and purity and an uninterruptible communion with the Creator.

And since, for angels such as Darien and Stedfast and tens of thousands of others—as well as men and women whose souls had, in death, left bodies no longer able to sustain life, souls that would be sent either to heaven or hell—time essentially did not exist, neither of them was bound by its conventions, nor enslaved by any mere clock.

And what both angels witnessed would not be at all like an instant replay but, rather, history as *it was unfolding!*

It was an invigorating ability, a cherished privilege.

CHAPTER 7

Angels could become bored sporadically, and it was a tonic to them to get to see Martin Luther begin the Protestant Reformation, to watch as Christian organizations through the centuries became the first to start hospices, to set up orphanages, and Christian scientists discover scientific secrets that had remained hidden for so long.

They were able to do this because they were present when God created the universe and all the planets, and it was His glorious Mind that gave absolute definitive order out of chaos, not some mere chance convergence of cells in a disorderly evolution that was unrelated to any master Architect.

"Remember what that famous comedian said some while back?" Stedfast spoke.

"How could I forget?" Darien told him.

Darien happened to pass by a luncheon at the Beverly Hilton Hotel that was being given to honor a legendary humorist. Normally he would have paid no attention, but this one was attended by the man's wife whose parents had been devout missionaries to China decades earlier.

He turned to her and said, "It is possible that, one day, I can believe as strongly as Jayne does in the Bible and God and Jesus and all the rest that means so much to her. But I haven't come as far as that, frankly. Let me tell you where I have arrived at present, because none of us knows what the future holds."

And he went on to give this explanation why, eventually, he had to come to believe in God, even if not as "evangelically" as his wife.

"I learned years ago that there were two absurdist notions competing against one another in the arena of thought," the humorist spoke. "One was that this world, the universe, all the rest, you know, came about by accident, that the exquisitely perfect pattern in a butterfly's wings, in a leaf, even in a snowflake, were products of chance. I have seen traffic in Mexico City, Rome, and elsewhere. *That* is a product of chance, ladies and gentlemen!"

People laughed, and he paused until they had stopped.

"Funny but true. Now there was, I discovered, this second notion, an absurdist one, to be sure, that suggested this world, this universe, all the rest, came about by some central intelligence, the scheme of a being we shall name God—Someone who spoke, and out of nothingness came the advent of what we see around us today when we visit Yosemite, watch a sunrise or a sunset, see a rosebush."

He rubbed his chin, smiled slyly, and added, "Of those two absurd notions, ridiculous to the core, I decided that the *least* objectionable, the *least* nonsensical was the latter, that Someone of supreme intelligence had given us gravitational laws, an amazingly well-organized universe, a cohesive creation that could not, I repeat, could not have come about *accidentally*. That was the true absurdity!"

CHAPTER 8

Las Vegas, twenty years later . . .

A little child.

"Look at that," Stedfast said.

"I am," replied Darien. "I am looking, and thinking of what Jesus said."

"About leading the little ones astray?"

"That is exactly it, dear friend. It would be better for those who have done so that they not have been born or that a millstone be hung around their neck and that they be cast into the deepest sea."

Young life, innocent children, patently impressionable, reacting to all that their senses told them—sweet little children were at the mercy of their parents *and* those who were seeking to influence the ones in whose homes they would live for many years—looking, absorbing, learning.

"So pitiable . . ." said Stedfast.

"It is more than that," Darien added with great reluctance. "It is surely the tragedy of the ages."

Adam and Eve sinned.

Then Cain followed in their footsteps. And his children after him. So on and on and on through the ages of time until—

"Poor little children," Stedfast spoke, close to sobbing. "I want to wrap myself around them and protect every last one."

"And so does their heavenly Father."

"Oh, yes! Think of His pain as the children are corrupted."

For many, that process of corruption would begin in their homes. A father drinks. A mother has a "casual" affair.

And what about the parents who were otherwise quite moral but were drawn to Las Vegas because of the new emphasis?

They were tired of Disneyland, Knott's Berry Farm, Universal Studios, and Magic Mountain.

And so Las Vegas became more attractive.

They would no longer have to leave the young ones home or hire a baby-sitter. Sons and daughters could be brought along.

"If they have a budget for gambling, and stick with it," Darien observed, "they can rationalize that it's no different than spending nearly a hundred dollars at some theme park. Take that money and spend it at the crap tables or in the slot machines. They cannot tell the difference."

Stedfast was especially depressed.

"But look at whose pockets the money is going into," he pointed out, "evil men who also promote drugs and pornography as well as prostitution businesses."

Evil men . . .

Both angels saw these foul creatures, the flesh-and-blood specimen, *and* the demonic creatures controlling them, mixing with fathers and mothers who seemed as clean-cut as the Beavers and Dobie Gillises and the other symbols of American families and American youth of another generation.

"If I were Italian," Stedfast opined morosely, "I would want to rise up."

"There would be bloodshed."

"So be it! I would want to rise up, however bloodily, against the mafioso because, over the years, the mob has become so entrenched in Brooklyn and Chicago and elsewhere."

The angel shivered as he contemplated those images.

CHAPTER 8

"The mobsters are like a cancerous growth among decent *Italian* families, Darien, spreading so rapidly that it is almost impossible to think of anyone who *is* from Sicily or Palermo or Venice or any other place in Italy as *not* being involved with La Cosa Nostra. If you are Italian, you are suspect."

"But the mobsters do not care," Darien said. "As long as they can control their own world, little matters to them in terms of what happens beyond its boundaries. The rest of the planet can go to hell."

"Literally."

"Yes, literally. I was not cursing, Stedfast."

"I did not think you were."

Both angels were distressed. They could watch the start of the deterioration of yet more families—a deterioration wrought not by sex or drugs or booze but gambling as people did so, in many instances, for the first time.

"Just that one ten-dollar bet opens the door," Darien said. "Just that first dollar at a one-armed bandit . . ."

They saw something that made their pain even more intense.

Parents *not* leaving their children at some kiddie-oriented amusement but taking them along *into* the casinos.

"Can they not see?" Stedfast moaned.

"Blindness has been an affliction from the beginning of time," Darien told him. "It can take many forms. People who are born without their eyesight can learn to cope as well as those who lose it from an accident later in life. But blindness of the human spirit, the soul, and, as well, blindness of the intellect, that is another matter, indeed it is, for this is a blindness that can be far more devastating than the physical kind."

Little children were being held lovingly in the arms of dangerously stupid mothers or fathers, exposing their offspring to the neon glitter that was part of a carefully conceived *atmosphere*—once again courtesy of Vincenzo DiCosolo. Little children, eyes wide, taking it all in, fascinated by the color, the sounds, the perceived excitement, seemingly little difference between this and the other family resorts.

"Daddy!" a son asked. "Gimme a quarter."

And the father did just that—lifted his boy up so that a little hand could place the coin in the slot, but this lad needed more help than just that; he needed help with the lever, to pull it down, to—see if he had won.

He did.

In place of that one quarter, a dozen others were spit out by the bandit. Eager little hands grabbed them and a fresh young face broke into a smile.

"What could be wrong with bringing a youngster some joy?" Stedfast asked as he watched this happen.

"In twenty years, that child will have become an adult," Darien answered, "an adult who had a favorable gambling experience, and nothing will stop him from commencing a fateful journey, taking another step, followed by another, and ultimately—"

Stedfast sighed, the image all too powerful, the waste of a soul all too tragic.

In twenty years . . .

The millstone was gone, the child became a man "hurl'd headlong . . . to bottomless perdition."

CHAPTER 9

There is no soul. . . .

It was at first a disconcertingly eerie sensation.

This sense of rampant and unquenchable soullessness, eerily akin to what an all too experienced and depraved Oscar Wilde just a century and a half ago described when he wrote, "Misery [born from despair] wakes us in the morning and [masquerading as] Shame sits with us at night."

. . . shame sits with us at night.

Even someone such as he, so thoroughly adept at the indulgence of various manifestations of perversity with other men, could never begin providing those words necessary to illustrate what the two unfallen angels sensed as they continued briefly in Las Vegas—the siren-like "glamour" of the town attracting any men or women who wanted excitement in a nihilistic world, excitement edged with the possibility of sudden wealth, the satisfaction of needs that instead would only be exacerbated by this den of deception, instead of eliminated altogether as it coyly promised.

Stedfast stood in one of the most extravagant casinos, invisible to all who entered with expectant smiles only to leave often with nervous, haunted expressions freezing their faces into what seemed like premature death masks.

"What deluded lost sheep!" this angel muttered.

The other angel told him, "Yes, I would know. They are flocking to damnation but none realize it or, knowing that this is so, they have signaled their willingness to eat, drink, and be merry regardless of the consequence of tomorrow."

"It is the middle of the summer," Stedfast pointed out, "and people are wearing as little as possible."

He hesitated, thinking, wondering. After all, the normal temperature should have been well over a hundred degrees.

And yet—

"It seems so cold," Stedfast spoke.

So cold . . .

Not even as severe as the chill of an Arctic winter, bleak and—

Worse, something far worse.

Darien could not have agreed more.

"You have observed correctly," Darien agreed. "But we are not feeling anything like the temperature indicated by a lowly thermometer."

Stedfast was puzzled.

"Then what is it?" he asked. "I have seldom felt like this."

After the warmth, the transcendent warmth of heaven, virtually anything else would have seemed disconcerting, but at least, after so much experience, these two angels arguably were accustomed to what earth had to offer.

Until now.

Until that insinuating chill.

"Before, Stedfast," Darien reminded him, "there *was* a time, yea, two times, three times . . ."

"Are you certain?" his fellow angel asked, yet uncertain. "I don't—"

"Be calm. Search your memories. It has been our blessing or our bane never to forget anything. Once you realize this, you will know the nature of what it is that disturbs us both this day."

"I still—"

If Stedfast had been like humankind, he would have snapped his fingers in sudden recollection, and blushed a bit as well.

CHAPTER 9

"You mean—?" he asked.

"Yes, I mean exactly that," Darien assured him, "as the first of the three, as the one that God could no longer spare from his judgment."

Stedfast had to admit his own stupidity.

"I should have known," he groaned, embarrassed, the memories now as vivid as the fiery destruction itself. "Sodom and Gomorrah . . ."

Stedfast began to muse about the end of those twin cities.

"You know, this is something that has never occurred to me before," said Darien.

"Tell it to me, friend."

"The flames, the molten rock, the rest of it?"

"Yes, I think you and I have always assumed that it was God's judgment from heaven, and I still believe that."

"Then on what are you cogitating?"

"I ponder . . ."

Stedfast's reflection was intense as he thought back to that incendiary moment when Sodom and Gomorrah were engulfed.

"Where the flames came from?" he wondered. "God could have ordered them out of thin air, as it were, right?"

"Yes, Stedfast, he could have done that."

"But consider this possibility."

"Go ahead."

"What if—?"

The images flooding his consciousness were staggering.

"I cannot think of them any longer," Stedfast said.

"Let me share this burden," Darien told him. "Let me help you, my comrade."

"All right . . . here is what I see. I see the barrier between earth and hell being swept aside for that instant, that instant only, and the flames of hell reaching up and submerging Sodom and Gomorrah, reducing it to blackened rubble."

"And demons among them, Stedfast, foul beings thirsting for new conquests, searching out the dying, their soon-released souls."

"And dragging them screaming to damnation!"

"What an awful sound!"

Darien had never heard another that was worse.

"The sounds of a thousand hardened hearts being rent open to face the truth, and being condemned by it for eternity."

Both were exhausted by that image, neither able to say more for what in earth terms was nearly an hour.

Stedfast had been praying silently but now he asked Darien, "There is more, is there not?"

"Oh, yes, sadly yes."

"Another center of depravity, flaunting its perversions."

"Every bit that."

Stedfast thought for a moment, then came up with another one.

"The Castro District in San Francisco . . ." he offered.

"Sodom and Gomorrah were not worse. And there are other places like it, centered as they are on degrading behavior, dangerous behavior, behavior that is an affront to any society that values decency, normalcy, that would eschew such moral filth if it were not spiritually compromised."

Darien smiled as he added, "Are you coming closer to the truth now?"

Stedfast was fully alert by then.

"At that abortion clinic in Boston where it was just a rather routine job for the entire staff, each baby dispatched with a coolness and efficiency that made us both quite ill of spirit. I remember above all that pile of—"

Fully formed bodies in miniature . . .

Stedfast shook himself as he realized where the insightful prodding of his comrade was leading him.

"No soul," he spoke. "This, like the others, is a place of utter soullessness. Is it an outpost for hell?"

"Oh, yes, Stedfast, it is every bit that. It is a portal through which so many sins entice, and all of it presided over by a single evil man."

The other angel did not have to ruminate about who that man was.

CHAPTER 9

"Vincenzo DiCosolo."

"Yet if he were to perish, as brilliant as he has been, the craven mobsters behind him would find someone else. While his death would set them back to a certain extent, the world he created could go on as his legacy for quite some time to come before it needed another man at the helm."

Stedfast was troubled, and said so, having learned that absolute candor between angels allowed Satan no haven from which to attack.

"I cannot believe he has *no* conscience," he spoke. "Perhaps we could reach him, change him enough to—"

Darien rarely interrupted his friend but this time he did, because he knew the Creator wanted them only to stop very briefly in Las Vegas on the way to Atlantic City.

"We should be going on to the East Coast as soon as possible," he remarked, "but I think it is important for you to see what Vinnie the Bear is like when he is not being polite or charming, the mask he dons for government officials and mobsters alike."

In an instant they were inside his luxurious home just inside the Las Vegas city limits, an extraordinary mansion, with eight bathrooms, ten bedrooms, three kitchens, an indoor heated swimming pool, and a great deal else.

"His favorite pastime is watching child pornography," Darien said, "when he is sure that his wife is not home and the household has the night off."

"He is a—"

"Yes, he is. And among the many associations, clubs, and other organizations to which he belongs is the one he never brags about: Boy Love International."

"No more," Stedfast pleaded, disgusted, a being of complete purity confronted by a man of complete depravity.

"But, surely, you must know that knowledge is one of our greatest weapons against the master of deception."

"All right, all right. What else must I see?"

"Where he goes when he is not in the limelight."

"And where is that, Darien?"

"A special multi-roomed suite on the top floor of one of the town's most prestigious hotels."

"What goes on there?"

"You will have no need for explanations once you go inside and see for yourself. Then you will know why Vincenzo DiCosolo is one of those rare individuals whom our heavenly Father has given over completely to a reprobate mind."

Vinnie the Bear never went to that floor before midnight. His duties at the casinos kept him busy elsewhere.

And the night the two angels followed him was no exception.

As Vinnie and his bodyguard, Rocco, got off the elevator and headed down the hallway to the single door at the end, both were grumbling about being tired.

"Why tonight?" Vinnie remarked. "Business is a little soft. We're not being run ragged after all."

"Those meetings in the morning . . ." Rocco reminded him. "All the pressure's got to you."

"You may be right. But it was worth the trouble."

"You said it, boss."

He wanted more access to drugs and hookers. His customers were demanding full service, and mob-mandated restrictions were rankling him.

"The young bucks don't mind," Vinnie said. "It's the old-timers who continue to resist, blathering on the way they do about morality."

"You were smart though."

"Thanks. I had to do what I did. What choice was there?"

What Vinnie accomplished was backroom agreements with the younger mafiosi about generating a sustainable drug flow.

"And the women," he had insisted. "Those Asian broads are in demand now. We can import them through San Francisco and Los Angeles, and then hire private planes to get them to Vegas."

CHAPTER 9

The young Italian up-and-comers were eager to get some action. Often, they were reined in by the predominantly aging dons but getting wise in the process. What the old men did not know would never hurt them.

"Until they find out . . ." Vinnie had warned ruefully.

"That will never happen," a good-looking twenty-five-year-old named Tony Graziani pledged.

"Salvatore, for one, is crafty, you know. It isn't easy to fool him."

"But his age is against him. He's forgetting things. He can be tricked. I know. I have done it."

"You sound real trustworthy," Vinnie observed.

"I am until it gets in the way."

Vinnie knocked on that one door. Someone opened it, and he and Rocco stepped into the suite.

The two angels, unseen, joined them.

"I fear that we have stumbled into an outpost of hell itself!" Stedfast spoke a bit tremulously.

"I have the same suspicion," Darien agreed.

In an instant, both were wishing that they had not gone inside because what they saw might as well have been plucked right out of hell, what they saw had all the ingredients of a demonic hub.

A planning room . . .

A room in which every foul and obscene action that could be promulgated throughout Las Vegas was being carefully planned.

"That sound," Stedfast told Darien, both angels tensing as they heard it.

Familiar.

The skittering sound of cloven feet.

"This is a hive," Darien said.

A hive was a central place for the meeting of demons, a nerve center. And Vinnie the Bear was deeply involved.

"Yet he does not know," Darien added. "He honestly does not know. He is under the most severe spirit of delusion we have seen in some while."

Stedfast had to agree.

In that room was a madame, the most influential one of all of Las Vegas.

Vinnie wanted to make sure she was in on all the plans, that she had a sufficient supply of girls.

"If you don't, I'll get some slant-eyed chicks from the Far East," he warned her. "They perform well."

The madame, a woman who weighed well over two hundred pounds, did not need to be convinced that Vinnie was serious.

"Now get out of here!" he bellowed.

Next came a black man, this man tipping the scales at three hundred plus.

"The drug supply," Vinnie said. "Any problems?"

"I got my homeboys working overtime. We won't let you down."

"Better not. The dons hate blacks who make promises but can't deliver."

This dealer knew better than to explode in front of Vinnie. He was patient, waiting for a chance to get revenge, on his turf, on his terms.

"You're the boss," he said. "Anything you need, whenever you need it. I got direct lines to Chicago, New York, Los Angeles."

"But not the Colombians, understood? If I find you playing with them, I'm gonna chop off your fingers, and make you eat each one!"

"Understood, boss."

"Now get out of here!"

There were others in the room, one dealing in pornography, another who was a chief of police, a third who had certain unions in his back pocket.

"We're all together, right?" Vinnie asked.

"Right!" they shouted in unison.

Vinnie was glad to hear this. His power evaporated if the mob bosses were to decide that he did not have everyone bribed.

No soul . . .

"Darien!" exclaimed Stedfast.

"Yes, friend?" the other angel replied.

CHAPTER 9

"Their souls . . ."

"What about them?"

"That eerie feeling we have been having . . ."

"Oh, yes, really quite awful, I agree—too much for us to endure for more than a short while without going back to the Creator disconsolate, worth very little to Him in that state, until we had fully recovered, helped by our fellow angels."

. . . helped by our fellow angels.

They all had experienced such moments, encounters that were so bizarre and filled with the basest iniquity that, as creatures of total good, they could not endure total evil.

"Sodom and Gomorrah . . ." Darien muttered. "Las Vegas is so much like these places of degradation. And Atlantic City will become the very same."

Atlantic City was central to the master plan of Vinnie the Bear and those others who were benefiting from the spread of gambling. Las Vegas was almost a cliché. It had been around so long that it was a barometer for anything, except in the blatant attempt at image-softening by turning it into a family resort.

. . . they have sold their souls.

That truth unnerved Stedfast whenever he encountered it.

"Sold . . ." Stedfast added. "Purchased by the merchants of damnation."

"All of them—certain police officials, the madame, the pornographer, the drug dealer, everyone who has anything to do with the mob. Unless they repent, they are headed to hell for eternity."

"Darien, I remember . . ."

"What do you remember?"

"A funhouse."

"A funhouse? You are an angel. I can only wonder about why in the world would you go into a funhouse?"

"Curiosity perhaps, wondering why human beings would deliberately subject themselves to being scared."

"What is it that you uncovered?"

"Part of it was an exhibit called the Mouth of Hell."

"How realistic, friend?"

"Very much so, in a *papier mâché* fashion, the slight odor of sulfur, artificial flames spewing from this garishly painted giant mouth, and in the abyss-like darkness beyond, the sounds of screaming, moaning, and bloodshot eyes just barely visible."

"Very strong, very real, as you say."

"The same here," Stedfast spoke, "but Las Vegas is not simply a carnival show *representation* of the Mouth of Hell. . . . it *is* that!"

Even Darien could not speak just then, looking at what were, in that context, those constantly arriving souls who, by their presence, were signaling a dangerous flirtation with damnation, right up to the mouth of a mad kingdom, and then stepping in, letting hell surround them with its enticements, men like Vinnie DiCosolo who were no more than stooges for the Prince of Darkness—"a dreadful hell," as Isaac Watts called it, "and everlasting pains, there sinners must with devils dwell, in darkness, fire and chains."

"It is only a matter of time," Darien said with sadness so complete that he knew they would have to leave instantly.

"Hell . . ." Stedfast muttered, "'the bloodcurdling mansion of time, in whose profound circle Satan himself waits, winding a gargantuan watch in his hand.'"

And then they were gone, unfallen messengers of heaven, leaving behind those who would stand for hours at a mechanical one-armed bandit, oblivious to quite another bandit, the leader of them all, real and perverse and evil, who had already stolen from the seduced damned their most precious possession of all, and given in its place nothing, nothing whatsoever.

And then they were gone, unfallen messengers of heaven. . . .

CHAPTER 9

Leaving evil behind them always frustrated both angels. They wanted to cleanse any human being they met, any town or city they visited, leaving behind instead a place of purity and decency.

It seldom happened.

Evil was entrenched, at places like Las Vegas and New Orleans. Evil, though, seldom came across as itself. Its "look" was rehabilitated and made appealing.

And neither angel had to look very far to find this truth displayed. It was given full-cover treatment in a publication that was part of what the Los Angeles Times *offered Sunday after Sunday, its magazine section showing a pleasant shot of a leading Las Vegas gambling industry figure and the attractive female then-mayor of the town.*

But what were these two smiling about?

According to the article inside the magazine, Las Vegas gambling had a stranglehold on the state's economy.

Everything revolved around it.

Young people were dropping out of high school or failing to go on to college in ever greater numbers because the casino interests were paying top dollar to anyone willing to work for them.

But Mirage CEO Steve Wynn and Las Vegas mayor Jan Laverty instead were quoted as worrying about the town's "image," and hoping to soften it so that it could be made palatable to everyone.

As the writer of the article, Tom Gorman, stated, "Selling a city that profits on both deception and perception . . . can be tricky."

Gorman went on to point out that those with an increasingly heavy financial stake in the ongoing success of Las Vegas for the foreseeable future claimed that they were winning the battle, and yet their alleged proof about this included only the fact that a group of Southern Baptists once held a convention there, and that some ninety thousand Mormons lived in and around Las Vegas.

Darien and Stedfast regretted this.

"That one particular group makes a mistake of judgment is only evidence of how powerful the demonic influences are in and around Las Vegas," he spoke. "Considering how many Christian groups are in existence in the United States, it is specious at best to spotlight a single example, and not back up that contention with many others across the theological spectrum."

PART III

Evil enters like a needle and
spreads like an oak tree.

Ethiopian Proverb

Six months had to pass before gambling was approved by the voters of New Jersey. Bret Erlandson was funded by a group of Christian businessmen and became a principal anti-gambling spokesman.

He took part in debates.

He was interviewed by television news commentators.

The Christian press triumphantly featured article after article on him, covering every aspect of his life but especially why it was that he was devoting so much effort to defeat gambling.

"I go wherever my Lord leads me," he replied more than once, "and I do whatever it is that He asks of me."

The interviewer—a Ted Koppel clone—asked sarcastically, "Oh, you are in direct communication with Him, I gather."

"Any man, woman, or child can do the same thing," Bret replied.

"And what is the same thing?"

"Find God."

"Find Him and engage in a conversation?" the interviewer asked, thinking that he had a hook for a story, which perhaps would, at the same time, go a long way toward discrediting Bret Erlandson.

"That is what prayer happens to be . . . in the original language, it means conversation with God."

"Do you ever hear audible explanations?"

"No."

"Then you can be imagining things, am I right? What you want God to say is invariably what He tells you. Show me where I am wrong."

And so it was, the case being constructed against this man as an extremist who should not be heeded by more sophisticated people. . . .

CHAPTER 10

The old woman was named Sophie.

She was white, overweight, with gray hair that kept falling out.

Sophie existed only on the barely adequate income from her late husband's pension and her Social Security check. She did have a few dollars left over each month, but not enough to do anything more than "splurge" now and then on some extra video rentals or perhaps a dinner out one or two nights. Otherwise her life had become predictable, with no sparkle whatsoever left in it.

Every so often she had afternoon tea with Ruth, another longtime resident in the barracks-like apartment building which had been home for nearly ten years.

"Gambling may be wonderful," Sophie was saying one day as she and Ruth sat on the balcony both shared since their apartments were side by side.

She had paid attention to all of the favorable reports and virtually ignored the negative ones, believing only what satisfied her desire to have gambling at her doorstep. Like most people in that area who voted for gambling, she could hardly wait for the games to begin, with little concern for the underlying reality.

"I *need* this," she told someone else when the possibility arose some time earlier. "I need this desperately."

Sophie was quite pitiable as she spoke, a woman who was an "ideal" candidate for the fleecing that gambling always wrought upon the unwary.

"Why?" the other individual asked.

"All my life, I seldom had what I *really* wanted. Is it so wrong if I finally have *something?*"

The woman with whom she was conversing could hardly disagree.

"You could become addicted, though," she said a bit hesitantly, not wanting to burst her friend's bubble at that point.

"So what?" Sophie replied. "At least I'll be happy. Am I happy now? I think you know the answer to *that* question."

. . . gambling may be wonderful.

Her mind was brought back to the present.

"You bet!" Ruth replied. "It could be fun. After all, how much of *that* do you and I have anymore?"

"At our ages, well, I sometimes forget what fun really is!"

"But think of this: You could be having fun one minute and become wealthy the next. Isn't that something?"

"I see nothing wrong in taking a few dollars now and then and playing the slot machines or shooting some craps," Sophie added. "All we'd have to do is skip a few videos or a meal out occasionally."

Both women were more and more warming to what they thought gambling promised for their lives.

"What about that man?" Sophie asked.

"The one who has been trying to stop gambling from ever coming to Atlantic City?" Ruth replied.

"I think he may be one of those ranting Christian fundamentalists; you know the type I mean."

"I'm not going to let people of that ilk control what I do."

"That's the way I feel," Sophie told her.

"There's going to be a public meeting next week," Ruth remembered. "Let's attend it, okay!"

Sophie nodded vigorously as she declared with gusto, "We'll take this so-and-so on, you and I."

CHAPTER 10

The two women talked for a few minutes longer, then returned to their respective apartments. For Sophie, it was a step back into loneliness. She had leased the apartment not long after her husband died, for she could not endure being alone in the bungalow that they had shared for more than ten years. Too many memories were assaulting her every moment she would spend inside the house, for it reflected a period of their marriage in which she saw her beloved dwindle day by day, until he weighed only sixty-five pounds, the victim of a smoking addiction that eventually ravaged him.

"How I miss you," Sophie said out loud as she sat on the little sofa in one of the three small rooms that comprised the apartment. "I mourn you every day. But I'm killing myself doing it."

She paused for a moment, consumed by sorrow and regret and the melancholy of those dreary days.

"I watched you wreck your body. . . ." Sophie said, images of a skeleton with skin stretched over it rising to the upper reaches of her mind, "yet I'm doing the same thing, eating the wrong foods, not getting enough exercise, spending all my time indoors because I can't afford a taxi to take me any place special. Dear Ruth has a little more money coming in, but she doesn't get out much either."

She was speaking, she knew, to nothing but the empty air—something she had been doing a great deal of lately.

"Nobody pays much attention to an old bag like me," she went on. "I have no one left but Ruth."

Darien and Stedfast were in the apartment with her just then, but she could not see them. They did not have permission from God to take human form, but they could nudge her with a thought now and then.

Trust God.

"God?" she said angrily. "What does He have to offer? He took my Albert from me and now He has plopped me here in this prison. Why should I pay attention to Him?"

You once did.

Sophie chuckled sarcastically.

"I once thought I could trust Him with my life," she shot back.

You can.

"I can, but I won't," she added.

It's not too late.

"It is for God!" Sophie shot back.

Darien and Stedfast left that apartment, and decided to walk to the Atlantic City that had been attracting people since the 1890s.

"Why can't we do more?" Stedfast asked. "If we materialized in front of her, that would have to startle her."

Darien was not moving.

"Listen!" he exclaimed.

Stedfast did, listening as God spoke to them both, and when He was done, they had no more questions about Sophie.

"Even that would not change her mind," Stedfast mused.

"According to God, yes," Darien agreed. "She is too embittered. Her heart has been hardened. She is the reason why she remains alone, except for Ruth. Sophie trusts no one else. People sense that about her. There are few human beings less attractive than someone turned so sour."

"That sounds awfully hard."

Darien admitted that it did.

"But it is the truth," he continued. "There is in this modern society that you and I have been seeing around us a reluctance to *confront* the truth, but, rather, people are interested instead in escape, running away as though that will take care of everything."

"An escape from the truth," Stedfast spoke, "and together with that, an unwillingness to accept any kind of real responsibility. Sophie is suffering loneliness because she has given herself a life of isolation and bitterness."

"So sad . . ."

"The prison she spoke of was one she constructed around herself. She could free herself anytime. . . ."

Darien looked back at the apartment building.

"She is looking to gambling for that," he suggested.

Though Stedfast wished it were otherwise, he could only concur with his comrade's statement.

CHAPTER 10

"Will she win any money?" he wondered.

"It does not matter."

"What do you mean?"

"Whatever the amount, she will put it back on the gambling tables and into the slot machines because by that time, she will have become an addict."

"Sophie is going to become enslaved to drugs?"

"Not that kind of addict," Darien remarked.

Suddenly, it occurred to Stedfast what his comrade was talking about.

"A gambling addict?" he asked.

"So seriously that Sophie will be driven into the maelstrom of a tragedy far more than any that she has known thus far."

"Worse than watching her beloved husband go from a robust two hundred pounds to sixty-five."

"Oh, yes, Stedfast, though she will surely carry those pathetic images with her to her grave."

"What could be worse?"

"We will have to wait and see."

"And we shall."

The fate of Sophie was just one of the dramas the two angels would encounter as they visited Atlantic City.

A tapestry of lies, deceit, and corruption on a variety of levels. . . .

There were others that would be played out before them. In only one instance were they granted permission by God to assume human form. But that time had not come upon them as yet. They needed to see more of the transformation of Atlantic City.

Transformation. . . .

How total the deception, how little people realized that Atlantic City would not become a kind of palace that people from everywhere could visit, and look in awe as they spent their money, and then left.

Not a palace at all. . . .

But rather, a kind of purgatory being turned into a kind of hell.

CHAPTER 11

Bret Erlandson was getting ready for the meeting at city hall.

He was nervous.

Young, handsome, charming . . .

But little of that mattered now. He was going to face people eager to cut him to ribbons, people drawn by the scent of his "blood."

It promised to be one that would not be soon forgotten by any of those men and women who happened to be in attendance, for he intended to bring up something that would create outrage but also skepticism.

"Molly, Molly . . ." he said as he sat in the dining room of the split-level house that his wife and he had lived in since they were newlyweds.

Molly, Molly, he repeated in his thoughts. *How deeply I love you. I would die for you, my dearest. One of the wonders of being married to you is not just that we think so much alike but that when we disagree, we seldom deteriorate into any destructive arguing that threatens to explode our relationship.*

Bret sighed to himself.

Oh, we argue sometimes but love is there, love is always there, whatever the circumstances, not meanness or any attempt to win the argument. We both are interested only in truth. And we always discover it together.

He smiled as he looked at her.

The Lord has been gracious, he told himself. *Though I don't deserve you, He has chosen to bring you into my life, and you are the greatest blessing of all.*

He was slipping into momentary reverie then when her voice brought him back to the present.

"You sound so tired," she told him, her once-long blonde hair gone, and in its place a new "look" that was much shorter.

"Working at the bank, manning the phones in the evenings, stuffing envelopes," Bret told her, "sure I'm tired. Aren't you?"

"Not as much as you are. I'm helping you because I love you."

"Gambling isn't as much of a concern for you, is it?"

"Not really. I figure if people want to ruin their lives, let them, just so long as I live mine properly."

"I respect your right to feel as you do, but, Molly, that's the same head-in-the-sand approach that Christians had early on when liberalism was beginning to creep into pulpits around the country back in the 1930s. And don't we have abortion clinics everywhere because Christians preferred to leave it all in the Lord's hands?"

Especially after thinking as he had been doing, Bret regretted those words and their tone, and knew that Molly was right when she said that he sounded very tired.

But she would not allow herself to become angry because she knew the pressures her husband had created for himself, and she did not want to add to these.

"I respect you," she said simply, "and I love you, and that's all that matters, as far as I am concerned."

Bret smiled, and reached across the table to hold her hand in his own.

"As long as we have each other," he told her with great affection, "you and I can get through anything."

Tears were starting in his eyes.

. . . you and I can get through anything.

That was what had helped them survive in the past, the knowledge that their marriage was providential, and, yes, they would survive financial lows, emotional stress, whatever else would be leveled against them.

"What about Annie?" Molly asked.

"She makes it worthwhile. I'm fighting to keep this area where we live as safe as possible. I don't want too much traffic. I don't want an influx of gangsters and drug dealers and any other scum."

"I think she knows this."

"A seven-year-old is aware of things like that?"

Bret could not be so certain of that, but if Molly was right, then it confirmed what he had suspected about their daughter for a long time, that she was someone very special, intelligent, perceptive.

"Our daughter is," Molly said. "She's always loved you, Bret, but lately there's something else as well in the way she acts toward you."

"What is it?"

"Respect. She may not know exactly why, I admit, but it's there."

"How can you tell?"

"The way she looks at you. It's subtle, of course, but there just the same. And I think that's wonderful, really wonderful."

Bret tightened his hold slightly on her hand.

"I cannot begin to imagine what I would do if I ever lost you," he told her. "You are my life, Molly."

And so it was between them . . .

Darien and Stedfast were deeply touched by what they saw. After misery and death on an Indian reservation, after greed and perversity in Las Vegas, and the occultic stranglehold on New Orleans, they were ready for a family united by love, ready for the joy of honest relationships rooted in decency.

"If only those elderly ladies could *see* now the man they referred to with such distaste and sarcasm," Stedfast suggested.

"It might not make a difference," Darien countered. "Instead they could be filled with jealousy, and that is another emotion which can be a tough taskmaster."

"Are you so sure?"

"Only our Creator could be *so* sure, my comrade. I can give you nothing but my conjecture in this case."

"Sorry," apologized Stedfast. "I loathe writing those women off. It goes against everything for which I feel I was created."

"I know what you mean. How could I feel differently? But the truth is that they are charting their own course."

"Like lemmings?"

"Very much so . . . hiding toward the edge of a cliff, blind to what will happen to them when they go over it."

"I yearn for heaven again," Stedfast spoke wistfully.

"But we must hide here, for as long as the Master wishes."

"Oh, I know, Darien, I know that well enough, but when you are living in the midst of perfection, anything else seems such a trial."

"A young family and two old women . . ."

"What can we do to help them?"

The two angels knew only that they would stay until whatever their mission proved to be was fulfilled in the way Almighty God wanted.

CHAPTER 12

Darien and Stedfast could have gone straight ahead in time to that evening's confrontation between Bret Erlandson, with his supporters, and their opponents lead by Vincenzo "Vinnie the Bear" DiCosolo.

But they did *not* do this.

Instead they both felt led to get an in-depth look at what pre-gambling Atlantic City was like, to see a painted lady before her makeup was changed and neon lights strung through her hair.

The first section of town that the two angels visited was the worst: the once fabled Inlet. An area of town that had been, at the turn of the century, highly regarded, fashionable and vibrant, a place to which the wealthy of that era flocked regularly, elegant horse-drawn carriages mingling with the few expensive automobiles that could only be afforded by the upper class, since Henry Ford had not as yet introduced the concept of mass production for the public at large.

Glamorous restaurants were plentiful.

Public parks were large and managed with meticulous care.

And people could walk through the streets at night with no serious threat of rape, murder, or robbery—the very crimes that would lay a blanket of violence over the Inlet within a few decades.

No longer . . .

The wealthy had been replaced by typical skid row derelicts having no place to sleep but on benches or given over to convulsing in gutters.

Townhouses and other residences, once the posh summer homes of well-to-do visitors, had been ruined over the ravages of many years and were now pathetic, broken-down shells, often empty but when occupied, they housed more than one family—sometimes as many as three which were crowded into living space meant for a single group of husband, wife, and a couple of children.

Rut-filled asphalt streets.

Cracked sidewalks that were little more than cement ribbons covered with dog droppings.

And the odor of poverty hanging over everything and everyone.

It was not something that could be explicitly defined, but it smothered the Inlet—an odor of excrement and dust and rot, perhaps like the interior of a tomb, an odor of despair if that could be imagined, despair that everything was dying, that there was no longer any hope, that Atlantic City was fast becoming a ghost town during the winter, propped up only by the fading hope of each summer season.

"Death . . ." Darien observed. "There is death here."

Stedfast agreed.

"The town is paying for its sins," he said, "for years of corruption at every level of government. Elected officials paid off by mobsters; members of the police department being slipped money to overlook a betting parlor here and there, bookies a key part of the underworld of Atlantic City."

"And what about the brothels which flourished here more than in any city except New Orleans?"

"Why . . ." Stedfast pointed out, "not even Los Angeles in the 1930s could top Atlantic City in that regard!"

"No vital industries, a seasonal employment flow that meant a considerable number of low-paying jobs during the summer but virtually nothing during the stale winter months of attrition."

Darien was struck by the irony of what they were saying.

"Probably words that will be said tonight by those who want gambling in Atlantic City!" he exclaimed.

CHAPTER 12

"Atlantic City needs help or it will die," Stedfast added, "if it is not basically dead already."

Gambling loomed as the magical answer, an approach not just to delaying the funeral but to resurrecting the patient altogether.

"But it is a resurrection of the body only," Darien spoke figuratively. "It will be like a mannequin in a store window, giving some semblance of life but a false one, a corpse dressed up to look like a living human being."

That image was right on the mark.

Throughout the Inlet, mostly black children acted like those of other districts in the Southern New Jersey region.

Yet there was a difference.

A big difference.

A difference that the two angels were sure would be used to good effect by the casino interests.

Poverty.

These children wore ragged clothes, old and dirty with holes and tears in them. Boys and girls were ripe for disease.

And crime.

Many would one day feel the tug of making considerable sums of money by selling drugs on street corners.

Along with their lives going down the drain, they would take others with them to the pit of hell.

They would link in with Colombian drug lords or mafioso rebels fighting the old-line dons who hated the use of drugs for profit. But the young ones did not care. Making larger sums of money illicitly was all that concerned them.

One day this dichotomy between the old-line gangsters and the young Turks would explode secretly, with more killings in a matter of months than there had been in decades. The aging dons still clung to a morality that favored so-called "victimless" crimes: prostitution, pornography, gambling.

Drugs were out.

"We can't destroy kids!" one powerful don declared. "We shouldn't even be considering doing such a thing. Is there no decency left among us?"

That sounded odd to the two angels when they first heard it.

. . . is there no decency left among us?

The angels knew that these dons believed their stand was a "righteous" one. Whatever the outside world might think of La Cosa Nostra, the morality it espoused required definite strictures. Adultery was out, at least adultery with another mobster's wife. Pedophilia was one of the most emphatic taboos, for the same reason as was drugs sold to kids in schoolyards or anywhere else.

But the young Turks were drawn by the lure of hundreds of millions of dollars that could be made from enslaving the young.

"How evil the human heart!" Stedfast spoke, sounding even more melancholy than usual.

"Try getting *their* sons or daughters into drugs, and if they caught you, you would be tortured and killed almost immediately, unless they wanted to prolong your agony," Darien added.

That was actually what would later start a gangland war.

One of the elderly dons found that his grandson had become hooked. He traced the pusher back to an up-and-coming young mobster whose contempt for old-line "values" was well-known.

The resulting murders led directly to retaliation, and that round of violence spawned another.

Yet the Federal authorities did little to stop it.

"If average Americans only knew what was going on behind their backs!" Darien exclaimed.

"They would rise in insurrection. . . ." Stedfast offered.

"Undoubtedly."

This little known war pitting one mob group against another was hushed up by those in the Federal government who were on the Mafia's payroll.

"As Hoover did during World War II," Darien said.

CHAPTER 12

"But there is no patriotic reason this time," Stedfast pointed out.

"There is."

"But what could it be?"

"Drugs."

"The old dons promised to join the war against drugs, putting themselves in an adversarial position with the Colombians, if the FBI adopted a hands-off policy toward what was happening in the underworld, with one exception."

"What was that, Darien?"

"The old guys needed better firepower since they found out that the young Turks had been stockpiling the latest weapons."

"And the FBI agreed?"

"To every demand."

"Nobody would believe that if it *did* leak out."

"That was the beauty of it as far as the Mafia dons were concerned."

So clever, so demonically clever . . .

CHAPTER 13

This was to be the most important meeting of their lives, drawing to it scores of people whose futures would be directly impacted by gambling.

A meeting destined to be right at the center of an enormous moral and spiritual discussion . . .

In fact, take away both the moral and the spiritual, and gambling would abruptly become a nonissue.

Was that an exaggeration?

Perhaps it might have seemed so at the time, at least as far as flesh-and-blood human beings were concerned.

And yet for angels Darien and Stedfast, there was never any doubt that it was valid—valid beyond anything those at the meeting could have imagined.

But then these two beings, choosing to remain invisible as they did, were aided by a kind of divine hindsight that always proved most extraordinary, being able as they were to journey to the future and then back once again to the past as they were doing in the course of their Atlantic City assignment, one of many that involved exercise of this time traveling gift, not on some frivolous whim at all but, rather, abiding by whatever the wishes were of their blessed Creator, the One who set the path of their travels called Angelwalk according to certain definitive boundaries, beyond which neither would ever go, the sort of restrictions imposed as a result of this becoming, long, long before, one of the principal reasons behind Lucifer's rebellion, since he was demanding back then the removal of all impediments of any kind to the exercise of his own gifts.

As a result he suffered the condemnation of *dêponere* from heaven, and he was never given the ability to travel Angelwalk himself. He was bound by the conventions of time and space much like flesh-and-blood human beings were, all the while knowing that his previous comrades could go backward and forward in time at will, so long as they continued to obey Almighty God.

. . . continued to obey Almighty God.

How Satan hated the implications of those words, for he harbored the ever-growing conceit that God should honor *him,* that his Creator should step aside and allow *him* to take over the throne of heaven.

"I shall win this war!" Satan declared again and again, era after era, to the other fallen angels, those duped by him into switching masters, from God to himself, from divinity to pure evil.

Satan would be there at the meeting in Atlantic City, unseen, and in attendance, at his side, were many fallen angels ready to influence those who were wavering.

"I shall get what it is that I desire here!" he declared. "My loyal Vincenzo DiCosolo will not fail me."

Satan wanted gambling. Satan needed gambling. Gambling was ideal for him—yet another hook that could be thrown into the lives of people whom he wanted to control. Give them gambling, and Satan had one of the most compelling obsessions of all. He would use this, as he used pornography, drug addiction, and alcoholism to dominate the unwary. . . .

CHAPTER 14

The meeting considered pivotal to support for gambling in Atlantic City, as well as the opposition movement trying to keep it out, was being held in the ballroom of one of the largest of the resort's old-line hotels, in itself a striking reminder of what had been happening over the years.

The anti-gambling forces were maneuvered by virtue of the very setting, a factor that did not occur to them until it was too late to change the site.

Bret Erlandson blamed himself.

"I should have known," he told his wife Molly as they were getting into their family sedan for the drive across the Albany Avenue thoroughfare into Atlantic City.

"Maybe so," she agreed, "but they have committees and consulting firms and layer after layer of people on their payroll. You can't be expected to cover all the bases that they are able to deal with."

"Doesn't that mean this attempt to keep them out is doomed?"

"Not at all. David did bring down Goliath with a stone, remember?"

Bret was glad that Molly had wanted to go with him. Just having her by his side would give him the encouragement he needed.

After entering Atlantic City, they passed by the high school they had both attended since they were born and raised in Ventnor as well as Margate suburbs, sharp contrasts to the Inlet section.

"We had some good times back then," Bret said as he pointed at the several-blocks-long, faintly English-style building where they had spent so many hours of each day, five days a week, for four years.

Neither went to college because they were hired by local businesses almost immediately out of high school. Bret went to work initially at the venerable Chelsea Title and Guaranty Company, and Molly got a job in a law firm with offices that happened to be in a building right across Atlantic Avenue from him.

"Did we do the right thing?" he asked absent-mindedly as these memories surfaced in familiar territory.

"About what?" she wondered.

"College."

Molly had thought in pro-and-con terms about that very matter every so often but always came to the same conclusion.

"The money would have been a problem, remember," she said. "We don't come from well-heeled families."

Bret nodded, then told her, "You're right, of course. I still don't see what we would have learned that could have helped us later."

"And think of the environment," Molly added with confidence. "How badly would our faith have been battered, I mean, with some of those professors that I keep hearing about even now?"

That had been a worry from the start. They could gain a higher education but damage something else of greater importance.

"We did the right thing," Bret remarked, "and yet, sometimes I just can't help wondering if—"

"Shush," she said, placing two fingers on his lips. "Keep your mind on what we're going to face in a few minutes."

As usual, he knew, she was right.

Just ahead was Pacific Avenue.

Bret turned the car left onto it, passing the Knife-and-Fork Inn where the two of them liked to eat whenever they had sufficient extra dollars to spend.

CHAPTER 14

He noticed the lack of traffic.

"Another mistake," he murmured.

"What is it this time?" Molly asked.

"The time of year."

"We should have resisted having this meeting in the winter, right?"

"Right!"

During the summer, Atlantic City showed some spark of life. Conventions poured into town. Tourists jammed the Boardwalk. The Steel Pier was open, and featured reasonably top-flight entertainers. Concession stands were selling everything from hot dogs to cotton candy to James' salt-water taffy.

No one minded that the queen of resorts was looking seedy around the edges. Somehow that added to the charm.

But after Labor Day, the shutting down process was well-nigh immediate. And a short while later, Atlantic City, like some aging bear with battle scars all over its body, crawled into a figurative cave and slept away the winter.

Bears had an advantage.

When hibernating, they were unseen. They just disappeared.

But Atlantic City was still on view, and without the sounds of crowds, without the cheap banners that were thrown up everywhere at the start of the summer season, it could be seen for what it was, and what it was saddened year-round residents.

Darien and Stedfast saw them sitting out on their narrow porches, middle-aged or older men and women, looking at the few passersby from row houses on Chelsea Avenue and elsewhere, these aging buildings dominating the scene.

"They are thankful for one circumstance but leery about it at the same time," Darien spoke.

Thankful for one thing, the relative quiet of that dormant time, but otherwise bored, both annoyed by the influx of traffic during the summer and buoyed by even a temporary infusion of life . . .

"They just exist!" Stedfast exclaimed.

"Not much more than that," agreed Darien. "And, of course, these are the people the gambling supporters will target."

"Satan does his work well."

"Much of the time that is the case. Consider what we learned in one of our forays into the future."

"Are you thinking about the Internet?"

"That I am, yes, indeed! Congratulations, Stedfast. You seem to be more perceptive than ever."

"It is your encouragement, Darien. Not all angels do as they should in helping their comrades."

"That is very true."

He fell silent briefly.

"Is something bothering you?" Stedfast asked.

"Yes . . ."

"Will you share this with me?"

"You and I both lost friends when a third of the angels of heaven joined with Satan in his rebellion."

"Yes, it was terrible. I pleaded with so many not to be duped by Lucifer, but they would not listen."

Angels forgot nothing.

They were extensions of God.

Their Creator could forget only sin after it had been washed away by the shed blood from Christ's sacrifice at Calvary.

"So did I," Darien recalled. "They were blinded by his magnificence and his intelligence. They could not see past these."

"You still have not told me what is bothering you."

"How many other angels *almost* joined with Lucifer?"

Stedfast had not considered such a question before. The implications of it astounded him

. . . how many other angels almost joined with Lucifer but held back?

Both realized that only God had the answer, and He had never chosen to raise that issue before.

"It matters little now, I suppose," Darien speculated. "After all, we have never seen any hints of an impending second Casting Out."

"They would be banished from heaven only if they manifested their allegiance for Satan."

Sudden realization flooded through Darien, so compelling that he could only assume it came directly from God.

"And that will never happen!" he declared.

"Can you be sure?"

"That I can, dear friend, that I can."

"How so?"

"Because of what all of us, ten thousand upon ten thousand, have learned about the devil since that bleak day in heaven."

"When the original ones left with him," Stedfast said, "they had none of the truths we have seen since then."

"They went with him on blind faith of a sort," Darien agreed, "faith that overshadowed any loyalty they felt for their Creator."

"And now none can ever break away, it seems, even though they are aware of the death, destruction, perversity, and other parts of the legacy Satan has left behind him wherever he has gone."

"How awful it must be for them! Knowing what they do about themselves and their leader, knowing that they are entrapped for eternity."

What images!

The sight and sounds of shrieking beings as they writhed in a lake of fire that would never stop burning . . .

"We knew so many of them," Stedfast recalled morosely. "We had beautiful communion along the way, communion that was so blessed it seemed that *nothing* could shatter it, that nothing could—"

Satan was stronger in that regard.

The emotions he was adept at generating in vast numbers of fellow angels who were soon to be fallen like himself—emotions strange to them since they had known only purity from the moment God had created each one—were nevertheless intoxicating, at the start, anyway. Pride, a thirst for power, a desire to unseat Almighty God and make Him share His throne with Lucifer—these were some of what he introduced into heaven and how he seduced thousands of angel into joining him—emotions once so alien and yet powerful, irresistible to the point that they would follow the archangel anywhere in order to help him achieve what they now also wanted for themselves.

"Like gambling," Stedfast offered.

"Oh, quite true, quite true," Darien agreed. "Fallen angels were addicted to Satan the way human beings can become to gambling."

"No wonder gambling has become so successful. Satan wrote the original blueprint for this deviltry."

"And tonight, people will find themselves in a position to choose between righteousness and a pastime right from the pits of damnation!"

There was no sense of exaltation in the way Darien spoken. He knew already that any efforts to stop gambling were doomed. Yet the people in the meeting hall were not privy to such knowledge.

For them it would be a genuine fight.

On one side was energetic, dedicated Bret Erlandson, who basically represented the Christian community, as well as concerned people of other faiths for whom ready assurances would not be enough.

"How can we *ever* believe them?" remarked one man who was an accountant. "They will make the bulk of all the money. Of course, they'll have answers that *sound* good. What else is new?"

It seemed that no one from that side of the issue was naïve enough to be duped by the pro-gambling interests. They knew all too well the pernicious nature of this multi-billion-dollar business, and the sort of individuals behind it, like those in the tobacco industry whose profits grew only as the number of smokers escalated. The more people smoked, the better the tobacco executives liked it. Their extravagant salaries were paid on the backs of men, women, and children who ultimately would develop some form of ill-health—either lung cancer, emphysema, or any of the myriad other ailments stemming from the root cause of cigarette smoking, not to mention pregnant women who continued to smoke despite the warnings of the impact of nicotine and such on their unborn children.

CHAPTER 14

On the other side of the gambling debate were those individuals with profits in mind. Gambling was a business, a slimy and foul one, but a business run much like any other, with presidents, and chairmen of the board, and vice presidents, assistant vice presidents, directors of finance, and all the rest of the long list of individuals who have sold their souls in return for a steady job, as it were.

"Gambling is a business of lies," Darien said as he waited in the hallway outside the room where the meeting would soon begin.

"Through to its core," agreed Stedfast.

"Promises are made, promises are kept but *only* to that handful of individuals who ever win big as they gamble."

"It is so obvious," Darien added, sighing.

He pointed to the people filing into the meeting hall.

"So many of them are completely blind," he said.

"If gamblers were, suddenly, to start winning more often than they lose," Stedfast remarked, "the industry would be bankrupt quickly. But it is making huge profits instead. Which means that the number of gamblers is growing astronomically. What other answers could there be?"

"If a man spends all his savings in a casino, do you hear the owners weeping over this poor soul?"

"Money that goes directly into their bank accounts."

"Bank accounts controlled by underworld entrepreneurs."

"But you and I are hardly alone in realizing this," Stedfast observed. "That is why Bret Erlandson is fighting so hard."

"And yet he will lose."

"Yes, he will."

Both angels knew the emotional, psychological and, yes, spiritual devastation that this man would feel, to *know* the truth, to see it so very clearly, but then to come up face-to-face with people so blind that they see little or nothing of it.

"Can you imagine how much of an impact that will have on him?" Darien suggested, as though by saying those words, he was drinking deeply of some kind of poison.

"All too well."

"And there is so little you and I can do."

"We can whisper into his mind. We—"

Stedfast lapsed into silence.

Just then, they heard from inside the meeting hall that the evening's activities were now beginning.

Both hurried to their posts.

CHAPTER 15

Hundreds of people took up every seat in the meeting hall, which was part of a hotel that had been around since the turn of the century and seemed like so much of the rest of Atlantic City, old and musty.

On a raised platform, sitting in folding chairs, were Vincenzo DiCosolo, Bret Erlandson, Mayor Arthur Aron, and Police Chief Ray Branson.

Vinnie was the first one to speak.

"I think Atlantic City should have gambling!" he said as though he were leading a political rally.

Many in the audience raised their voices in support, while a few decided to boo him.

"Gambling will be good for Atlantic City," Vinnie went on, oozing a sleek confidence that would have rung alarm bells for anyone who had had experience dealing with someone of his ilk.

Bret could not contain himself.

While the meeting was not billed as a debate *per se,* and there were no set parliamentary rules as such to be followed, interrupting your opponent the way he had just done seemed implicitly wrong.

But Bret was not letting that stop him.

"How can it be good for Atlantic City?" he challenged the other man.

"Money, Mr. Erlandson," Vinnie countered. "This town is dying. It is like a plant not getting enough water."

"So the ends completely justify the means as far as you are concerned?"

"Absolutely! If it means families having enough money to buy food, you bet I believe the ends justify the means."

"What about the morality of it? What about the spiritual bankruptcy that gambling encourages."

"Whose morality?" Vinnie continued. "Yours, Mr. Erlandson? You're a fundamentalist Christian. Why should we listen to someone like you? Why, I bet you would have been against school-teacher Scopes in the famous Monkey Trial earlier this century."

"Why should people's faith be attacked by the *theories* of a man named Darwin who, before he died, began to doubt what he himself had set in motion? He was brilliant, yes, and as his life started to ebb from him, he envisioned his theory running amok like some Frankensteinian monster.

"Some reports indicate that Charles Darwin became a Christian before his death and that he scribbled a recantation of his theory on a sheet of paper, and passed it to one of his associates who decided to destroy it rather than see all that his mentor was accomplishing ruined overnight."

Vinnie was momentarily taken aback, and seemed like a prize fighter whose opponent had gotten in an unanticipated solid punch on the jaw.

"But then this meeting is not about evolution, is it?" he went on, trying to regain the momentum.

"You were the one to introduce it, not me," Bret reminded him.

"And you have seized upon that simple statement of mine in an attempt to obfuscate the real issue here before us!"

Vinnie had been facing Bret but now turned toward the audience.

"We meet tonight not to debate the theory of evolution or fundamentalism but issues far more relevant to our lives, to our futures," he said, banging his fist down on the podium. "We have gathered together to decide whether a narrow-minded few can dominate what happens to the great majority of the rest of us."

CHAPTER 15

. . . a narrow-minded few.

Bret knew that he could not remain silent, and stepped forward.

"You are presenting yourself as one of us," he spoke. "Yet you have flown in to Atlantic City on your expensive private jet, with your entourage picked right from Mulberry Street in Brooklyn."

Bret had no idea what that would mean to the people listening to him, but he hoped some would draw the link to organized crime.

"That is an *Italian* neighborhood," Vinnie interjected. "Are you a bigot on top of everything else?"

"That is an Italian *Mafia* neighborhood," Bret shot back at him, spelling out his meaning. "Oh, I know, I know, gangsters have been a part of the Atlantic City scene for a long time. And I am equally positive that we have had drug pushers here before and prostitutes and politicians guilty of the most obvious chicanery."

He faced the audience without blinking.

"Does that mean we open the doors even wider and make Atlantic City and its suburbs a nest for that kind of scum? Do we throw our values out the window because we are uncertain about the future?"

He faced Vinnie the Bear again.

"Are you here to benefit Atlantic City?" he demanded. "Or to extend the influence of a so-called pastime that has ruined families?"

Bret did not let him interrupt.

"Yes, gambling will bring in lots of money but it will destroy many of you," he said, looking over the audience and making eye contact with as many men and women as possible. "It will hook retirees into throwing their pension checks away in the hope of sudden wealth. It will mean higher property values, of course, but that will cause escalating rents so that landlords can pay their taxes.

"The elderly will be hit again. Many will not survive. More than a few, in fact, will end up on park benches or at the Atlantic City Rescue Mission, driven to depending on the kindness of strangers."

Vinnie started laughing so loudly that several in the audience cringed a bit.

"Old wives' tales," he said. "There is less poverty in Las Vegas than in any other region of this country."

"You miss one point," Bret told him.

"And what might that be?"

"That Las Vegas was formed with gambling in mind, that *everything* in that town is structured with gambling as the nucleus. You and your crimelord backers—"

"Now wait a minute!" Vinnie shouted at him.

"No, mister, *you* wait!" Bret shouted back. "We can always regenerate the economic base of Atlantic City. We can make it a center of the pornography business, with marital aids stores and nude dancing bars on every block. We can adopt a hands-off attitude toward drugs so that pushers have greater freedom to sell their goods. We can make Atlantic City the gun capital of this nation."

His eyes widened defiantly.

"We can do all of this, and more like it, and, yes, a thousand times yes, *that* will bring in many, many dollars of extra revenue."

Bret faced the audience again.

"Is that what we want? To go the way of Sodom and Gomorrah? If so, how long can we expect God's judgment to be forestalled?"

Shouts of "No! No! No!" arose from the scores of people in that meeting hall as they responded to Bret's exhortation.

Vinnie knew that, so far, he was losing the battle. But he had been prepared for this eventuality.

"In just a short while," Vinnie told them, "I will be introducing someone many of you have seen on television."

As though on cue, a man entered the hall and strode to the podium, one of the TV preachers whose program was seen not only locally on one of the offbeat channels, but watched nevertheless, but through a hundred or more other channels across the country. Eventually he would be in competition with Jim and Tammy but, for the moment, he had the electronic church audience in the palm of his hand.

"These people are good honest folk," he said, his voice thundering over the loudspeakers. "They are running a business, that's true, but they are willing to give all of you concessions that amount to acts of generosity like few I have ever seen before now."

Nor was this flamboyant individual the only one whom Vinnie would march forward to champion the cause of gambling. Business leaders from within the Atlantic City community would join the parade.

"It would revitalize my furniture business," proclaimed one man.

"My construction revenues are down," said another. "I'm against the ropes right now. Taking part in the boom would save me from bankruptcy."

Others stood and told of hard times that the influx of gambling would solve overnight, elevating the quality of life for everyone involved.

Then elderly Sophie had her say.

"I live in a prison," she told everyone. "My pension and Social Security checks hardly last the month. When I do have anything left over, I go out to dinner or maybe rent some video tapes."

She was obviously annoyed and lonely, and not even Bret Erlandson could ignore her.

"These are the last years of my life," she acknowledged. "Must I spend them as I do now, with so little fun, just getting up each morning, my knees hurting me, my back hurting me? Sometimes I am so constipated that I have to stay in the apartment."

Her candor made this frail-looking figure a riveting one at the same time.

"Gambling would bring a little sparkle into my life," Sophie went on. "I would get out, meet people, maybe have a chance of winning enough money to rent a bigger prison."

Laughter.

"I could buy a larger TV, rent more videos, eat out more often. My wardrobe is old and musty like I am. I need some new dresses, shoes. Is it wrong to want a nice little bottle of perfume now and then?"

She turned and faced Bret Erlandson who was still on the raised platform at the front of the meeting hall.

"Why should *his* values be forced on me?" she demanded. "He is a Christian. So am I. Is his faith stronger than mine? Is it better? Does it give him the right to demand that I live the way *he* wants?"

Suddenly she seemed to be shedding a few of the years that encrusted that aging frame of hers.

"I think it would be wonderful to bring gambling to this town," Sophie declared. "There would be more money for schools, for public works. More people would have jobs, and most of these at higher pay than—"

She stopped, her face flushed.

Her friend Ruth made Sophie sit down and calm herself. Ruth then stood up.

"What if Sophie here has only a year or two left?" she asked. "Is it such a great sin that she indulge herself at a crap table or a slot machine? Why is *that* evil, as this man has been saying? If he sees it as evil, and I don't, does that make me the greater sinner?"

She pointed at Bret.

"You have no right!" Ruth exclaimed. "And I want you to leave Sophie and me alone to be happy any way we can!"

Bret got to his feet and started to say, "Don't you know what will happen? Don't you realize that your rent—?"

But he was not allowed to finish. Boos from the audience silenced him, and he had to sit back down.

It was over then.

And there was nothing more he could do.

Other speeches came, but from the pro-gambling side. Bret felt as though he had had his heart cut out of him. He possessed just enough remaining strength to stay in the meeting hall, avoiding the image of having been chased out by everyone's reaction to what Sophie and Ruth had said.

The future of gambling in Atlantic City was not determined by that one meeting.

There would be many more like it, and Bret Erlandson would put in an appearance at a fair number of these, but he knew that he was defeated; he knew that the gambling interests would win over the majority of voters; he knew that what he dreaded would become a reality, and all the Sophies and Ruths of that area, old and desperate and lonely, would get what they wished—they also were going to get what they never dared to imagine, and it would swallow them up like so much garbage.

Garbage.

That was how the insiders in the gambling industry viewed those who were giving them fat profits.

"They're fools!" one of Vincenzo DiCosolo's associates admitted to a friend in an unguarded moment. "We dangle before them prospects of instant wealth and keep hidden from them the possibility of either instant poverty or the slow, dripping kind that comes on them before they can stop themselves."

Vinnie the Bear cackled as he added, "And we are the only ones who earn the real money!"

The friend, another man about his age, was not surprised. He had known Vinnie for a long time. And yet the sheer exuberance with which all this was being relayed turned the friend's stomach.

After that luncheon meeting, Vinnie's friend returned to his own office elsewhere in Las Vegas.

"God help those people . . ." he muttered. "When Vinnie is done with them, they won't have much of anything left."

PART IV

Let none admire that riches grow in hell;
That soil may be best
Deserve the precious bane.

John Milton

It took months for the first indications of the real impact of gambling to sink in, not the impact that the promoters of it focused on but something else altogether—something that was not fully anticipated, a cold and cruel reality for those individuals who had campaigned hardest for the approval of gambling.

None of the warnings from opponents such as Bret Erlandson and others seemed to have been valid.

Hoopla.

Vinnie the Bear was adept at camouflage.

He knew how to divert attention from flaws and focus instead on virtues, if such a word could ever apply to gambling.

Celebrities came in by the truckload. The festivities were extraordinary even by show business standards.

Atlantic City was wrenched out of hibernation!

All the glitter was persuasive.

And when tax money from gambling started to pour in, politicians rejoiced. They had taken a gamble, no pun intended, and seemed destined to be thought of as heroes by those in Atlantic City who had learned to look at the future before gambling and recoil at the dismal scenes that came to them—scenes of greater poverty, race riots, a collapsing economic base, and much more.

CHAPTER 16

Initially Sophie and Ruth were delighted.

When the first casino opening was announced, they could scarcely wait, and were hoping to be the first customers on the first day.

"Wonderful!" Sophie said. "I can hardly wait."

"Yeh, but getting to next month will seem like forever," Ruth told her, completely in agreement.

"It's fun just *anticipating* going there."

"I'm glad people didn't pay much attention to that creep. I feel a migraine coming just thinking about him."

They had convinced themselves that he was a bad man, that he got his jollies trying to stand in the way of what people really wanted—which was what Vinnie the Bear intended, namely, that everyone swallow the propaganda that he and his mobster cronies had been spewing out since the beginning.

"Erlandson?"

The very name made her angry.

"Yes, him," Ruth replied, speaking with contempt that she had not disguised even at that crucial meeting.

"A fanatic," added Sophie.

"You bet he was!"

"Now you and I really have something to look forward to instead of just these four walls."

Gambling was presented as the key to a new life for the elderly as one of many groups that would benefit.

Money . . .

They stood a chance of winning huge sums of money but would never experience anything less than a good time.

"How many times are the two of us going?" Ruth asked, anxious to start making up a schedule.

"Maybe once or twice a month."

Ruth actually had in mind going to a casino once or twice a week, and hoped she could convince her friend to join her.

"No more than that?" she asked tentatively.

"Depends upon how much we win and lose," Sophie replied, the more level-headed of the two, it seemed.

. . . depends upon how much we win and lose.

The two angels who were standing there with them on the same balcony that had been Sophie's and Ruth's meeting place for so many years could only react sadly to what they were hearing.

"They are like sheep being led to a slaughterhouse," Darien spoke. "How tragic it is that they have been duped so expertly."

"And the crude, violent men who duped them have no concern for the havoc that they will cause in these lives and hundreds of others," Stedfast said. "I must try to do something, to put in a thought that they should be more cautious."

"Go ahead . . ."

Sophie closed her eyes, enjoying that early afternoon moment.

Warm.

The temperature was unseasonably high.

Pleasant breezes carried in from the Atlantic the odors of saltwater and those indefinable other ones from the sea—ancient odors that had been there before the resort ever existed, and would remain long after the two women were gone.

CHAPTER 16

"Feels good against my face," Sophie remarked.

"Yes, indeed," her friend agreed.

Noises, clanging, pounding . . .

Not far from where they were sitting, the two women could detect the sounds of construction mixing with that of seagulls swooping down for clams and other morsels that had been washed up on the famed Atlantic City beach.

"You can just tell," Ruth ventured.

"Tell what?"

"That Atlantic City is going to be reborn."

Ruth's eyes widened, the palms of her hands sweaty as she added, "And we're going to be part of it."

"A big part."

"They counted our votes, and now they've got to deliver for people like you and me, isn't that right?"

"It sure is," Sophie assured her.

"I feel as though I have a whole new lease on life."

"You're not the only one."

Another month.

That was all they had to wait after more than a year of anticipating, convincing others in their apartment building to support gambling by talking to them, handing out pamphlets, working the phones.

Stedfast was sure that he had found an opening.

What if those promises were nothing but public relations hype?

Sophie jumped, startled by a sudden thought that seemed to come from nowhere. Ruth saw how she reacted, and asked if anything was wrong.

"A terrible idea . . ." Sophie admitted, amazed that the thought would ever have entered her mind.

"What kind of terrible idea is that?" her friend asked, perplexed, but also intrigued, since her friend was acting quite differently that day.

"Me? You're . . . asking . . . me?" Sophie stammered.

"Yes . . . what do you mean?"

Sophie was very confused, not exactly an unknown state of mind for someone of her advanced age.

"About what?" she asked.

"You said something about a terrible idea."

"Oh, yes, I did. Sorry."

"Well, what did you mean?"

Sophie tried to get her nerves back together, as she said, "What if those promises were nothing but public relations hype?"

Ruth looked at her strangely.

"Why in the world would you say that?" she asked.

"I don't know."

"You don't know? I hope you're not getting cold feet. I wouldn't want to go to the casino without you."

"It's just that—"

Stedfast tried once again.

Do you realize who is benefiting the most from gambling?

Sophie was not taken so much by surprise this time. Even so, her hand was starting to tremble a bit.

"Are you becoming ill?" Ruth asked. "Your face is a little pale."

She was genuinely worried about Sophie since no one else in the apartment building seemed as smart as her dear friend was.

"I feel funny."

Ruth looked at her.

"What if mobsters *are* involved?" Sophie asked.

"I can't believe you're saying that! It sounds like propaganda from this Erlandson character."

Yet, to her credit, Sophie did persist.

"Isn't it a possibility, at least?" she asked pointedly. "I mean, all you have to do is look at Las Vegas over the years."

"Why now, Sophie?" Ruth wanted to know. "Why are you thinking of these things now?"

Sophie knew that the other woman had a point.

"Yes," she admitted, "it *is* strange of me, isn't it?"

CHAPTER 16

Ruth nodded her head vigorously.

"You bet it is. Now stop it, and let's decide on a reasonable schedule for being at the casino."

"Fine . . ."

They planned on once a week, and pledged to one another the discipline that would be needed to stick to this.

They went once a day.

And they kept on going.

Until a nightmare that neither of them could ever have guessed had seized both old women and did not let go.

CHAPTER 17

They went once a day.

And they kept on going.

Until a nightmare that neither of them could ever have guessed had seized both old women and did not let go . . .

It was a nightmare that Bret Erlandson had anticipated and tried to drum into the heads of anyone who would listen.

It was a nightmare that, while the elderly proved an easy prey, would not leave him unscathed.

And it all boiled down to one word: money.

This was the goal in Atlantic City and Las Vegas and on every Indian reservation and in every community where gambling was being conducted.

A world where twenty-five million dollars was a commonplace sum!

A world where someone's savings could be wiped out with a single roll of the dice, loaded or otherwise.

A world of smiles and bright lights and phoniness so apparent that it was almost laughable, like a bad TV sitcom.

"The obsessive love of money . . ." Darien spoke with obvious gloom as Stedfast and he stood outside the first of what would prove to be a variety of casinos built in Atlantic City over the next twenty years.

"A frenzied pursuit of it," the other angel agreed. "They try to use other words—pastime, fun, the rest—but money is what they are after, money that is not earned but which they hope will be handed to them."

People were willing to lose thousands of dollars to get a chance to win perhaps hundreds of thousands. What they seemed unable to grasp was that if the odds were in *their* favor, the casino operators would be bankrupt in short order. Chances that *customers* were on the winning side proved little better than one to three percent.

The two angels went inside. Immediately they were witnesses to a pathetic sight.

A heavyset man had just won five thousand dollars at one of the crap tables, and he was ecstatic.

"A loss for the casino," Stedfast observed, playing devil's advocate.

"It seems that way," Darien commented.

If the winner of all that money had simply cashed in his chips, and walked out of the casino, then it would have been a loss for the owners—five thousand dollars of profit down the drain.

He stayed.

And he lost that money plus another three thousand.

Unnerved, the man finally decided to quit.

"Here it is," Darien said. "The facts are there. And this little drama is repeated thousands of times a week."

Thousands of times a week, in Atlantic City, and New Orleans, and Las Vegas, and on Indian land in dozens of places . . .

"He lost two thousand dollars originally," Stedfast went over the figures. "So, he was minus that much. Then he won the five thousand. He was plus three thousand. Next, he lost the five, which made him minus two thousand. And, finally, he added three more thousand, bringing his losses for the day to five thousand."

"And it is seldom any different for others like him. Remember this: You could look at it another way. He *lost* ten thousand dollars but won back five. Every moment was engineered to have the outcome that way."

"The dice were loaded?"

CHAPTER 17

"It might better be said that the odds of anything that is gambling in Las Vegas or Atlantic City are set so that the casinos get at least ten cents of every dollar played, Stedfast."

"But I thought there were safeguards against that sort of thing."

"Only when the authorities are looking."

"How do the operators know when someone is going to be in the casino to check on them?"

"They are tipped off in advance. In a bureaucracy, nothing is spur of the moment. *Someone* knows. A corrupt system is controlled by gangsters who are bilking the public under the guise of 'fun.'"

The two angels wandered through that casino, and came upon Sophie and Ruth playing side-by-side slot machines.

Ruth had lost twenty-five dollars but won it back four times over. But that just coaxed her into playing again and again until her winnings were gone. She ended up with a loss of fifteen dollars.

Sophie did not win anything at all that day. Her loss was thirty-five dollars.

"Not a great deal of money," Stedfast spoke, knowing what his fellow angel's response would be.

"In just one day!" Darien exclaimed. "That would have been eating-out money for a month. Or video money. Perhaps a little of each."

Gone.

They would have to skip those little luxuries.

"You might think that they would stop at least until next month's checks came in," Stedfast reasoned out loud.

Neither did.

They dipped into their modest savings, and bankrolled another afternoon, two days later, at the same casino.

"Twice in one week," Stedfast said. "Already, that means they cannot rent any videos, or eat out for the rest of the month."

"And next week Sophie and Ruth will go to the casino two more days and lose at least as much."

"Spending *next* month's disposable income, as paltry as it is."

"But then there are just over two more weeks in *this* month left."

"More savings withdrawn. More lost."

"And then something that will happen just before they realize the trap into which they are falling."

Spotted . . .

Men whose job is to tag people like Sophie and Ruth passed on what had happened to their superiors.

"I think they are losing too much too soon," one of them said.

"I agree. Follow them carefully. See what bandits they are using the next time they visit. And fix it."

"How much, sir?"

"Let's see now. After each one has lost, say, twenty dollars, make sure they win three hundred."

Everyone was smiling.

"After that, we'll *own* those two old ducks!" the manager of that particular casino said, chuckling.

And "they" did.

For Sophie and Ruth, during their next visit, each lost twenty dollars at first, then both got "lucky" and found their one-arm bandits coughing up three hundred and ten dollars to Sophie, and two hundred ninety-seven to Ruth.

"I knew it!" they both shouted at the same time.

Sophie and Ruth decided to walk out with six hundred dollars-plus in winnings between them.

"Is that a problem?" one of the "watchers" asked his boss, aware that his job depended upon being alert.

The boss shook his head.

"They'll be back," he replied, "their kind return to the casino again and again and again. We got those old birds for thousands of dollars over the next couple of years, maybe more."

Their kind . . .

Two old women being encircled by birds of prey, their dignity gone, their common sense with it.

CHAPTER 17

They had become objects of derision even, at the same time as their deriders grabbed for their purses.

Someday, after their savings were gone, and they—

"How can you tell?"

"Vegas."

"The same thing."

"It happens there every day. It happens here. The odds are the same."

He was licking his lips predatorily.

"You see, we *control* them now, though they may never realize this," he spoke. "Perfect situation, just perfect."

Darien and Stedfast overheard everything. They quickly followed Sophie and Ruth back to their apartment house.

Save it . . .

Ruth was startled as that thought sprang up.

"Don't you think we should put this money away for now and wait until next month?" she asked.

"Why?" Sophie asked.

"We may need it."

"But we can use it to win some more."

"Or lose it all."

"There's always that chance."

Ruth hesitated, then said, "If we hadn't won this, we'd be forced to stay in our apartments and not go anywhere until next month."

"But we did win it. So what's the problem?"

Ruth was not as assertive as her friend.

"All right . . ." she acquiesced. "When do you want to go back? Tomorrow. Or next week?"

"Tonight."

"Tonight?"

"Yes, why not? We're hot today, Ruth, real hot. You know that! You can *feel* it just as I do."

She paused, frowning.

"We might not be like this tomorrow," Sophie added apprehensively.

"Seize the moment, girl!"

So, they returned to the casino and lost what they had won earlier in the day, plus another fifteen dollars each.

CHAPTER 18

The impact upon Bret Erlandson was quite different.

Fortunately, during the first several years, he had not allowed himself to fall into the trap of gambling, not after opposing it so stridently. But he was still suffering, in incremental ways.

The value of the Erlandson ranch-style home had gone up dramatically since the advent of gambling, from sixty-three thousand dollars to one hundred ten thousand in less than three years.

On the surface, that seemed to be one of the pluses that came along with gambling. Helping families build up their net worth was a principle goal of home ownership, and gambling hastened the process.

"See that!" Darien exclaimed. "The same old deception."

Stedfast could not agree more.

"Gambling seems to have put tens of thousands of dollars into the pockets of families in the Atlantic City area," he said.

"But then, watch what happens. . . ."

Property taxes.

The Erlandsons' tax bill went from twenty-two hundred dollars a year to just over five thousand.

"They are unable to get the advantage of all that extra value added to their assets," Darien remarked, "because they are not interested in selling the house."

"Yet their tax bill has gone up two and a half times," Stedfast added.

For the couple next to the Erlandsons, the difference proved all the more striking.

"We only paid sixty-two thousand for the house a few years ago," Emily Freeney said as she visited them for the last time.

"What happened?" asked Molly while Bret sat back, thinking of how prophetic his warnings had been.

Amazing.

That was the only description Emily had.

"It really was," she told them. "Yesterday, I was housecleaning, and happened to look out the window in the living room."

She had a curious expression on her face as she recalled that moment.

"What did you see?" asked Molly Erlandson.

"A huge all-black limousine! Even the windows were black. It just sat there for a few minutes."

"That must have made you *real* nervous!" Bret exclaimed, "given the reports of the influx of hoodlums into the area."

Emily chuckled over that. "Nervous isn't the word for it," she acknowledged.

Neither Erlandson had been home when this was occurring, and they both regretted that they had had to do some shopping at the same time.

"Take your time telling us," Molly told her sympathetically.

"It *was* quite an experience," admitted Emily.

She was gradually calming herself down as she continued, "Then this real tough-looking character, wearing a long black coat, gets out, and starts walking up the pathway to my front door."

"Was he carrying a semi-automatic rifle or a pistol or something?" Bret posed, deliberately melodramatic.

"None of those. He had an attaché case, brown leather."

Stereotypes reared up in Bret's mind.

CHAPTER 18

"With a gun *inside* it?" he asked.

"I kind of thought that, too," Emily confessed. "In fact I was getting ready to call the police."

"What happened next?" Molly asked anxiously.

"He rang the doorbell once, twice, a third time. I debated whether to answer it or not. Like a fool maybe, I did open the door a crack and asked this bald, wrinkled, fat little man—he wasn't any taller than five-foot six—what he wanted. Despite my misgivings, I did try to be as friendly as possible to him."

It was Bret's turn.

"What did he say?" he asked.

"'Your home,' he told me. 'I want to buy your house.' I replied that it wasn't for sale, and started to close the door. As I did, he opened the attaché, and that was when—I've got to tell you, I was ready to scream louder than an air raid siren."

It looked like a scene from a classic gangster movie, and Emily Freeney was right in the middle of it.

"Go on. . . ." Molly Erlandson prodded her.

She and Bret were putty in her hands as they sat, listening, tensely, waiting for the punch line.

"What was in the attaché case?" Bret asked.

No gun or any other weapon. Just—

"Money . . ." Emily continued. "Row after row of one hundred dollar bills. After showing it to me, he said, 'Cash, we pay all settlement fees, you have a month to move out . . . and we will get you a deal on any house you move to anywhere it happens to be.' My lips were numb but I managed to ask, 'How much are you offering?' He smiled crookedly as he told me, 'Four hundred thousand dollars.'"

Emily had to close her eyes before she continued her story. Her head was pounding. She was perspiring.

"That kind of money meant we could pay off the mortgage, all of our other debts, and plunk down cash for a house elsewhere!" she said, her eyes widening.

"But, Emily, to accept it requires that you do business with the mob!" Bret exclaimed in turn.

"Al and I both realize that that is a possibility."

"Then, surely, you're going to turn it down."

"We've accepted the money already. The papers were presented to us last night. We'll be gone in three weeks."

. . . we'll be gone in three weeks.

Emily was clearly conflicted but the deal was such a fast one, avoiding all the normal hassles of house-selling, that it would have been attractive under any circumstances; factor in the overriding element that they were getting at least six times its market value, and the lure became irresistible.

Emily and her husband Al both were Christians, yet they had succumbed to another aspect of the intrusion of gambling into Atlantic City.

"They sold out!" Bret exclaimed a few hours later. "How could they? They should have continued with us in this fight."

"The boys are clever," Molly told him.

"The boys?"

Bret had only vaguely heard that term before, and he was curious about his wife's use of it.

"The Mafia guys."

"Why did you call them 'the boys'?"

"A magazine article referred to them in that way."

"You've been reading about gangsters?"

"To know the enemy is to be armed against him, isn't it?"

Bret nodded in agreement.

"Absolutely," he remarked.

"Bret?"

"Yes, Molly?"

"Reminds me of *Invasion of the Body Snatchers.*"

"It's not much different than that, I have to admit."

"They'll try to blend in as much as possible. You can count on being invited over again and again."

CHAPTER 18

"Even us?"

"Oh, sure."

"That sounds bizarre."

"But it makes sense on a variety of levels. Opposition that is permanently nullified is part of why these goons are so successful. If they can't corrupt, they'll destroy. It's worked well for them for decades, maybe longer."

"Murder?"

"That's always one of the options for their kind. If you can't bribe your opponents or disgrace them, then you kill whoever is standing in your way."

"And what they'll really be doing is planning all their moves, figuring out how to expand their prostitution and pornography businesses and—"

"Just what we warned people about."

"But now the money's going to be spread around, buying silence and cooperation from one end of this section of the state to the other."

State officials were being corrupted at every level of government. Even in the governor's office, there were people swayed to the side of the gambling interests by promises of extravagant "soft" money donated to state and local campaigns.

In one of their steps forward in time, Darien and Stedfast had witnessed the uproar regarding Democratic fund-raising practices, and the transformation of the White House into a common roadside motel by the "renting" of rooms to major donors.

"It happens whenever outside interests want to gain influence," Darien pointed out. "And that was the case in New Jersey."

"Could top legislators *not* have known about the continuing mob influence?" Stedfast posed.

"Impossible! If Bret Erlandson knew, surely men and women higher up the ladder *had* to have known."

"Can we be sure?"

"Do we *need* to be, Stedfast?"

"I really would like to know."

"So would I."

The two angels went back in time about four years, but for them it was not a matter of time at all since time, as such, did not exist for angels. For these two, it was simply a question of "stepping" forward or backward. By doing so, they would be in the future or, just as easily, the past.

A room in a hotel near Trenton, New Jersey.

An elected state official was handed an envelope from a mobster named Sammy Domenicozzo, the number-two man in the Gambinelli crime family.

But the official hesitated.

"Worried about doing the right thing?" Sammy asked.

The official said nothing.

"Well, let me tell you what the right thing is here," this five-foot, seven-inch tough guy told him. "It means putting your beautiful kids through college. It means having a real nice home and a car that you can count on to work, not some old wreck that you're constantly patching up. The right thing is to make sure that you get home each night to your loving family without having your knees broken. I hate pain, you know. Ever had your knees smashed? It ain't pleasant."

The elected state official took the envelope.

"Every month," Sammy Domenicozzo assured him as the two of them stood. "For doing what?"

Pausing, he smiled knowingly before adding, "For making sure that nothing stands in the way of people having fun. Is that so bad?"

The official was convinced, at least he gave that impression, and he left that hotel room near Trenton, New Jersey, with ten thousand dollars in a side pocket.

"Everyone's morality is turned inside out," Stedfast observed.

"And it will get worse, though some people will claim that it's actually better for them," Darien remarked.

CHAPTER 18

"How *could* they do that?"

"We should go to a certain neighborhood. You will see quite clearly what it is that I mean."

In an instant, the two angels were there, on a street not unlike one of those in Little Italy, a section of Brooklyn, New York.

Midnight.

People were carefree, even serene.

"They seem not to have a care in the world, as the expression goes," Stedfast remarked. "And yet look at the hour."

"A turnabout," Darien acknowledged.

"But why *this* street?"

"One of the crime family's top lieutenants lives here."

"Not the don himself?"

"Further down on the ladder, but influential in any event."

"And he is responsible for the way people are acting?"

"Absolutely!"

Robberies in that neighborhood were nonexistent. There had not been a rape since gambling began. Husbands did not cheat on their wives.

"Strange . . ." Stedfast said.

"What is strange?" Darien asked.

"It is as though Christian morality has been imposed, not the threat of gangland retribution."

"Yes, it *is* curious. The various dons around the United States all insist upon the same code. It is a code of the most rigid morality."

"But selectively? Is that not right?"

"It is exactly right, my friend. They punish adultery but speak the worst profanities. They have the greatest concern about women being raped but think that prostitution is permissible."

"Contradictions or hypocrisies?" Stedfast posed.

"It has been this way for decades," Darien said. "Who knows?"

Those men and women who allowed the Mafia to control life all around them were rewarded with a crime-free mini-society of sorts that surely would stir the envy of law enforcement specialists everywhere!

CHAPTER 19

Angels Darien and Stedfast left the Erlandsons for a short while and came right up against another offshoot of the legalization of gambling. One that had never been thought of even by Bret and other opponents, but which those pushing for gambling knew all too well—knew and did not care.

Single mothers . . .

Especially those who were not well-trained in such areas as secretarial work, had never gone to college, and had no real business skills, yet they faced the responsibility of raising another human being.

The impact on them . . .

"How terrible!" Darien reacted. "Gambling supposedly offers them a new chance at building a decent life for themselves."

Supposedly. Always that word, couched in clever phrases, designed to deceive those who desperately needed hope.

"So long as they are willing to parade nearly nude in front of a lustful audience," Stedfast added.

"Think of their children. What hope is there for them?"

Many of the voluptuous showgirls were single mothers who worked at the casino ballrooms. They were not one bit different from those who were parading around on stage in Las Vegas.

"So wretched!" Stedfast spoke. "What these women feel they are compelled to do in order to survive."

"They are well-paid," Darien reminded him. "As always, money is the irresistible lure for them."

Well-paid and nearly nude—strutting around in the most erotically suggestive poses.

"Vinnie the Bear discovered a long time ago that sexually aroused men are inclined to gamble a great deal more after the stage show is over," Darien observed. "Having these women do what they do is as manipulative as that."

. . . having these women do what they do.

Some would go further than that, would meet men after they signed off for the night, men who would take them to motels where another show was put on.

"I fail to see the connection," Stedfast said rather stupidly.

Darien was patient with him.

"Their passions are surging, and they compensate by using one-armed bandits and throwing their money away at the crap tables."

"Like taking a cold shower."

"Very much so, Stedfast."

"So calculating."

"Everything is presided over by a Machiavellian genius."

"Is Vinnie as smart as that?"

"No, but his master is."

Both angels paid more attention to the showgirls on stage in one of the casinos, hoping to prod consciences that would force them to stop.

In the dressing rooms.

They went from one to the other, trying to tell them that they were not pleasing God by the way they earned money.

"Did you say something?" one of the dancers would say to another.

"Nope."

"I thought—"

"Wrong again."

CHAPTER 19

Dixie Dolley was the name of one of them. For a moment she seemed most receptive to what the angels were trying to tell her.

She had the dressing room all to herself. The other women had left on a break, to get a quick dinner, or gamble a bit.

But Dixie was too tired to move.

She just sat there, looking at herself in the mirror which was ringed by frosted light bulbs.

"How much longer?" she said out loud.

She had been one of the showgirls in Atlantic City since gambling had started. For a long while she had no problem defending her "profession." Then one day she had an encounter with a hooker who died right in front of her from a drug overdose.

"Get out while you can!" the hooker yelled at her.

"But I'm not—" Dixie started to say.

A few seconds later, the hooker was dead.

Nights later, in the dressing room, as she examined the way she looked, Dixie saw that her appearance was in fact much the same as a hooker, an overabundance of makeup, skimpy clothes, a growing hardness that made her look significantly older than her twenty-six years, yet still some sexual allure about her, enticing, suggestive.

See what is happening . . .

It was Darien who planted that thought.

Dixie turned sharply, "hearing" the angel with such clarity that she assumed it was someone who had entered the dressing room.

Empty . . .

She continued to be the only individual there.

"If only I *could* stop . . ." she said wistfully.

You can. Get up and walk out now. They will find someone to replace you in an hour or less.

She was becoming more and more nervous.

"I have no other way to earn a living," she countered.

You must seek another life.

"This is the only one I know," she pleaded.

Every week, she earned significant money doing what she did. That was what gambling provided for her.

And both angels knew that there would be no victory with Dixie.

She was grateful that they were gone, though she never learned who they were, or why they had decided to try and change *her* mind.

Even as she looked at herself in the mirror and wondered how much longer she could last, she also realized that there was nothing she could do.

"I am a mother!" she spoke. "I need to get paid more than I would waiting tables in some second-rate restaurant."

She looked at a photo of her daughter.

"How I love you," she whispered. "I would do anything for you."

Finally, she left for the night, her shift ended.

Out in the parking lot, the cool, clear air felt good inside her lungs.

"I'll make it through all this," Dixie Dolley announced proudly. "Yes, I think I actually will."

Her key did not make it into the lock on her car.

Someone grabbed her from behind and dragged her into the back of his van. Then a friend tied her hands and legs, before dismembering her body piece by piece.

Vincenzo DiCosolo was told what had happened minutes after the police discovered her body.

He was notably undisturbed.

"It happens in Las Vegas, too," he told a friend who was much more alarmed than Vinnie.

"Is that all you can say?" the other man asked, disturbed.

"What more is there? Look, gambling can bring riches, but it can also mean violence. I never tell the people I'm conning that, but it's true. Everything is at a high pitch . . . and passions are stirred. For some of us, that means sex. For others, it's taking a knife and cutting up some showgirl. That's just part of the price paid."

Vinnie the Bear looked at his friend, a cold tone to his voice as he added, "No big deal. Chill out, will you?"

CHAPTER 19

The other man did not do what Vinnie advised.

"In the end, is this what gambling has done to you?" he asked. "Made you an unfeeling monster?"

"Look, pal, we make people millionaires, we make them paupers. Millions of suckers lose billions of dollars. Do you expect me to cry over everything that happens to everyone who enters this fantasyland?"

His friend spat on the ground at Vinnie's feet, and started to walk away.

"Man, you'd better keep your mouth shut!" Vinnie yelled after the other man.

"Don't count on it," the friend shouted at him in just as loud a voice, "not this time, you sicko!"

Soon after that, in the privacy of his office, Vinnie made a call to Mulberry Street.

Darien and Stedfast asked God to allow them to return to heaven briefly. He had no objection, so that was what both angels did.

"We had to get some relief!" Stedfast exclaimed to Gabriel, one of the mightier in God's realm, who had just returned from fighting demonic forces in Bosnia, evil rampant in a region torn by genocide.

"You know," Gabriel told them, "it might seem that my mission has been the tougher one, but I have concluded that yours is proving to be as important, as necessary, as frustrating. I see men, women, and children dumped into mass graves. I see families split apart by war, the most unspeakable atrocities justified in the name of someone's view of God and race and whatever."

"It might as well be World War II all over again," Darien remarked.

"Or Uganda under the rule of Idi Amin. Or Russia under Stalin."

"Those who preach a kind of Utopianist doctrine have been awfully quiet lately, have they not?" Gabriel added. "The human race will evolve into a more humane species as time passes."

"Nonsense!" Stedfast exclaimed. "A millennium ago, there was the Inquisition, followed by the Crusades. A few hundred years later, the French Revolution provided

new evidence of a tendency toward barbarism during the Year of the Terror."

The three angels lapsed into silence, thinking of a race of beings to whom they were supposed to minister and suddenly filled with repulsion toward many of them.

PART V

Courage is like love;
it must have hope for nourishment.

Napoleon I

The more Darien and Stedfast thought about Bret Erlandson, the more they admired him, and the angrier they became toward his detractors.

"They were very scared—scared that he would be successful in derailing everything they had been planning," Darien said. "Now they are ignoring the man because they think he cannot hurt them any longer."

But now that Bret had lost, he could at least settle down and make the best of what was happening.

"Will he become complacent?" Stedfast asked. "And settle in like so many others, accepting the so-called inevitable?"

"Only God knows for sure," Darien replied. "I would like to think that, eventually, this family will move elsewhere, perhaps go to Colorado Springs where there is such a strong Christian community."

"That is a good idea. Should we plant it in his mind?"

"Yes, we should. Getting Bret Erlandson away from Atlantic City as soon as possible seems prudent."

"Is something brewing, something God has confided in you about?"

"Danger . . ."

"His life will be threatened?"

"I believe so, Stedfast."

"By the Mafia?"

"Yes, but not in the way you must be thinking, no strangulation by piano wire

or anything like that."

"What then?"

"You and I will have to wait, to see what evolves."

"Is he going to—?"

"I do not know!" Darien exclaimed with a rare touch of anger, and was instantly sorry that he had spoken like that, and asked the other angel to forgive him.

"Of course," Stedfast replied. "But I was being too pushy, too anxious, not willing to wait for the revelation of God's will."

"I know, I know, but it was wrong, this way I acted."

"Well, it is forgiven as well as forgotten, my friend."

"You seem to care a great deal about this man," Darien observed.

"I do," Stedfast told his comrade.

"Why?"

"Because of his integrity, and because his family depends on him. They seem so fragile in the wake of the gambling juggernaut. I would hate to see them ground up and spit out by it, oh, I would hate that!"

"That is quite true. I hope—"

Darien paused, his manner suggesting that a wave of great sorrow was sweeping over him.

"Have you been given insight by the Father?" asked Stedfast.

"I have."

"Is it as I feared?"

"Worse."

"Oh, no!"

And it was.

CHAPTER 20

Taxes . . .

These went up, yes, but were not all that was hard hit by inflation, but property taxes were symptomatic of what was beginning to happen, proving to be a crippling load for many of the families living in the vicinity of Atlantic City, families whose budgets were stretched *before* gambling arrived.

More . . .

The negative side of gambling.

Its supporters never acknowledged that *anything* negative could come from gambling, because they were too busy weaving a fantasy comprised of the so-called benefits of gambling, the rebirth factor, as it was called in the media.

Yet, along with the rise in taxes, there was a consequent escalation in charges from businesses in the Atlantic City area—the cost of goods and services jumped, since *everyone's* taxes were going up.

Ever larger numbers of men and women increasingly found themselves in an unnerving bind instead of what they originally conceived as financial gain, baited by men like Vinnie DiCosolo and others of his ilk, oozing out of the wicked underground of Mafia bribes, intimidation, and whatever else it took.

Busted . . .

Bret Erlandson's budget was busted.

Property taxes alone went from less than two hundred dollars a month to well over four hundred.

His utility rates climbed.

What he paid for food, gasoline, and a variety of other indispensable items quickly followed suit.

And he was not earning enough money.

So, Bret got an appointment with the president of the bank where he worked and asked for a modest raise.

"Can't do it," the man told him honestly. "Look, you know what has been happening around here."

That Bret did, yes, he did know.

Every bank in the area was losing tellers to the casino—men and women who were seeing their salaries go from not more than thirty thousand dollars a year to fifty thousand or more—just what was needed to keep up with the inflationary spiral that gambling caused, plus leaving some extra money for house remodeling, a new car, and the other goodies that such revenue allowed.

Banks that were part of national financial organizations could weather the loss of employees by paying enough additional money to their remaining cashiers, managers, and others to keep them from leaving as well—though even this tactic was hardly a cure-all, leaving as it did the threat of an exodus intact because the casino interests were not above raising what *they* paid for new employees.

But smaller banks, independent ones, either with no branches or just a handful, could not compete. They were stuck with paying employees what they could afford and, most of the time, that was not enough.

Bret had few options.

The most apparent one was that of selling the house and moving elsewhere. Yet both Molly and he had been born and raised in New Jersey. Pulling up deep-down roots was bound to be traumatic.

"And what about getting a job in another state?" he said as they discussed what to do. "Who knows what I'll run into?"

CHAPTER 20

"I could apply for something," she ventured.

Bret was opposed.

"I'm not saying you *couldn't,*" he told her, "and if it was something you really *wanted* to do, I would support you completely, but we have both felt that it was so very important for you to be a full-time mother, and not let some hired hand have any kind of influence with our youngsters."

"What do we do?" Molly asked plaintively.

"I'll go out and start looking for something else."

"After all these years of working for that bank . . ."

"It's a shame, but there's no other way to turn."

"But what is there around here that is worthwhile, Bret, yet not connected with the casinos?"

"Not very much."

That was the only answer he could come up with.

He could go to work for one of the other banks, but the pay scale would be little different from what he was getting already.

"What about opening up your own business?" Molly offered.

Bret hesitated, thinking about that briefly—at first not liking it because the risks were obvious, but then it started to appeal to him.

"I guess I've been thinking about that for awhile but afraid to acknowledge it as a possibility," he admitted. "But where would we get the money?"

"A second mortgage," she told him.

"The first few months are likely to be very lean."

"But we could weather that. Bret, an awful lot of people know you and would trust you to handle at least some part of their financial affairs."

"You may be right."

They spent a large part of the next week talking about Bret getting up an accounting business, and once the idea took hold, they staked out some time to look for an office on Shore Road, an active thoroughfare where walk-in business could be added to the kind that built from word-of-mouth.

Then they made up a budget that included every possible area of expense: office space; furniture; utilities; small ads in the local weekly newspaper; phone bill; temporary loss of income during the start-up period; much more.

Thousands of dollars.

But at least it would be an investment, an investment with the potential for ultimately easing their financial burdens.

"We could be independent," Bret said with more than a little excitement. "We could live as we have wanted to live, without worrying about having enough money to make it through the month."

A good idea.

Oh, yes . . .

That was what it seemed at the beginning, so this husband and wife made the decision to go ahead.

Bret gave his notice at the bank.

His boss tried to get him to change his mind, but the lure of a business of his own was too powerful.

CHAPTER 21

The devil had ways.

He could be charming or he could be quite maniacal in his pursuit of victory against his own Creator.

And in Vincenzo DiCosolo he had found the perfect front man, the best possible puppet whose strings were inextricably being pulled by the Prince of Darkness.

Vinnie the Bear DiCosolo found out what was happening with Bret Erlandson almost immediately.

Darien and Stedfast were astonished that he could have done so, and alarmed that he had been able.

"Where does this man's influence end?" Stedfast asked. "Where are his limits of influence?"

"We can answer that question by reminding ourselves where it begins," Darien reminded him.

In the pit of hell . . .

That was where it began.

They stood inside Vinnie's private office in the penthouse suite of one of the most elaborate of Atlantic City's new hotels.

"Any idea what this guy's going to do?" Vinnie asked the informer, jabbing a finger at him as though he was the enemy and not Bret Erlandson.

The other man nodded, never eager to disappoint someone as powerful as Vinnie DiCosolo.

"I just found out," he said.

"What did you find out?" demanded Vinnie.

The informer was smiling broadly as he replied, "Bret Erlandson wants to start a business of his own."

Vinnie was immediately interested.

"What kind of business?" he probed.

The other man was quick to answer.

"Accounting," he said.

Vinnie was rubbing his hands together, anxious to be able to confront an individual who was so well-equipped.

"Wonderful news!" he exclaimed.

"Why?" the informer asked.

Vinnie had learned to be patient with *some* people, those he needed to give him what others could not.

"Don't you see?"

"No . . ."

"We'll send him all the clients he needs."

The informer was flabbergasted, but he had been in and around the Mafia long enough to know enough that he should never be insulting to Vinnie who would not hesitate to order him a cement overcoat.

"I see . . ." he said simply.

"Any particular kind? Doctors, lawyers, CEOs?"

"It doesn't matter."

"And then what will happen?"

Vinnie looked like a man who had just been given a trophy for some outstanding achievement as he said, "When he's in deep enough, we'll spring the trap."

"We sure will."

Vinnie had been sitting, crouched, as though he was a predator ready to pounce if given the opportunity.

Now he stood and hugged the informer.

"We always get what we want, don't we?"

"Because of you."

CHAPTER 21

"Flattery will get you anything you want."

"It's true."

Uncomfortable over the possibility that he was being judged as insincere, the informer wanted Vinnie to know that what sounded like flattery was a fact—a fact of which not only he was aware.

"You got the boys together about Atlantic City," he said.

"That's true," Vinnie agreed. "I did."

"After all, how often do *they* agree on anything? At the beginning they were nervous, thought that it would cut into Las Vegas' business too much."

"Did it?" asked Vinnie, but already knowing the answer.

"Apparently not. Both locations are doing really, really well."

"About Erlandson?"

"Yes, sorry. He should be a pushover. All this noise about faith and honesty and the rest—I think it's paper-thin and very, very vulnerable."

Vinnie's enthusiasm was being stirred, so much so that perspiration soaked his clothes.

"I'm gonna own that guy mind, body, and soul."

The informer winced a bit, having seen Vinnie manifest this attitude before, and knowing what it always led to in the life of anyone he considered his enemy, anyone or any group who incurred his wrath.

"Is that what you want?" the informer asked. "You wouldn't settle for forcing him to leave this area?"

He paused, then added, "Think about that, Vinnie."

Vinnie did not have to do anything of the sort, no reason to think any longer about the answer to that question, for he had played this scene before, as the expression goes, and he knew it well.

"Is the pope Catholic?" he spoke confidently.

Darien and Stedfast overheard all of this, unknown to Vinnie, of course. They stood next to him, yet were not able to gain to his mind as they had been able to do with Bret Erlandson, because Vinnie was possessed while Bret was redeemed.

There was occasion for rejoicing.

Knowledge . . .

Now they knew what Vinnie intended to attempt, and they could alert the Erlandsons, so that that family could be prepared.

"We can warn Bret and Molly now," Stedfast spoke with jubilation. "How wonderful that is!"

For a change, Darien also felt optimistic about the situation.

"They *can* be on guard now," he added.

Both angels were to be with the Erlandsons, anxious to plant in their minds a warning—a warning that could aid the survival of a husband and wife whom they had grown fond of, and admired.

CHAPTER 22

Bret and Molly were planning the opening of the new business when a strange thought occurred to him.

"What if . . ." he said.

As soon as it occurred to him, he felt a chill over his body, and his face went pale in an instant.

That thought came from an angel, but he was completely unaware of this. It was a thought inserted with great gentleness into his mind by a being whom he had never seen but who shared God's love for him.

"What are you talking about?" asked Molly.

"I was thinking about the possibility that Vincenzo DiCosolo might try real hard to sabotage us."

Molly was amazed that her husband was giving the man any credit for that kind of power.

"You can't be serious?" she asked.

"I am," he told her. "Somehow I think he'll have to try. He is driven by ego, this guy, and it's urging him to do me in but good."

"You sound as though you believe that he can control everything," Molly, alarmed, suggested.

"Well, to be honest, we can count on his influence being more pervasive than most people realize."

Molly muttered agreement, since Bret merely confirmed her own fears about how devastating an enemy Vincenzo DiCosolo could be.

"Are we getting into some kind of war here?" she asked nervously. "That sort of thing probably stirs *his* blood."

Bret shrugged his shoulders. "Does it matter?" He placed a hand gently on his wife's shoulder and said, "We're on the Lord's side, Molly. Isn't that the only reality we should care about?"

"But the children . . . what about them?"

"I doubt that even Vincenzo DiCosolo would be arrogant and cruel enough to ever attack them directly."

That was not entirely what Molly had had in mind, and she spoke up, "But what if he destroys our livelihoods?"

"Then we go down another avenue."

She was half-laughing as she told her husband, "I wonder why all this seems so easy for you."

Bret's expression showed that he could not disagree more.

"It isn't like that at all as far as I am concerned," he told her. "Molly, I don't mean to sound casual at all. I just tend to be ready in my mind with other choices if one doesn't work out."

"You could have fooled me."

Bret rubbed his stomach for emphasis.

"My gut is rumbling now. My heart is beating faster. I have no idea what we're getting into."

Suddenly, Molly seemed close to trembling, a dark and cold feeling grabbing hold of her.

Bret's response was immediate.

"Then let's leave," he told her. "If you're starting to feel uncomfortable, that means a lot to me, my love."

"Leave?" she repeated.

"Forget about Atlantic City."

She was unprepared for him responding so quickly.

"Where would we go?" she asked.

"Colorado Springs. Yes, how about there? I've been hearing that the

Christian community there is growing rapidly."

"I've picked up similar information."

Bret had been to Colorado Springs for a banking industry convention three-and-a-half years earlier, though Molly was too sick at the time with the worst case of flu imaginable to go with him. He was impressed, especially with the Navigator's Retreat and the peace and quiet of its seclusion.

A castle.

Guests booked themselves at a charming decades-old English castle that had been reconstructed near the entrance by the original owner, a millionaire who built it as a special gift for his wife.

I loved staying there, he reminded himself, *and wished that Molly had been by my side, for she would have gone for it even more than I did.*

Years ago.

His mind was brought back to the present by Molly's voice.

"Someone as experienced as you could get a job in no time," she was telling him earnestly.

"With one of the ministries?"

"Sure! Isn't it worth a try, Bret?"

"You might be right."

He rubbed his chin before adding, "Could I sleep on it?"

"We both should. . . . Let's see if we feel differently in the morning."

"I love you," he said.

"And I love you, too," Molly told him. "Whatever we need to work out, we will, as always."

Bret stayed up a bit longer, suddenly uncertain, anxiety getting hold of his mind, and refusing to let go.

Be at peace, Bret Erlandson. Be at peace with whatever you do.

"What—?" he asked as he sat up straight in his favorite, well-stuffed chair, thinking that he had heard a voice speak to him from the semi-darkness of the family room, before adding: "Who's there?"

No one . . .

Only—

Silence, except for the sound of a dog barking outside, and the ticking of a clock in the hallway.

Nothing more.

But the thought remained.

Be at peace. . . .

Bret Erlandson went up to bed, strangely serene at that moment, even though a man who hated him was trying to destroy his life.

CHAPTER 23

"I think we are going to be very proud of them," Stedfast said.

"So do I," Darien agreed.

They had been spending the equivalent of weeks with their flesh-and-blood charges, planting a thought here and there, nudging the family along, waiting for God's instructions at each point.

And it all seemed to be worthwhile, this effort on the part of beings unseen. . . .

By noon, the Erlandsons had made a decision: They were moving to Colorado Springs instead of opening up a new business in the Atlantic City area. And they would go with a specific new mission: to set up a ministry dedicated to helping gambling victims and educating men and women everywhere about why the spread of all kinds of gambling had to be exposed.

And two persistent angels could claim credit for that radically different direction of their lives. Darien and Stedfast rejoiced when they heard of this, oh, how these loyal, loyal angels did rejoice that morning.

"A thought here, a thought there," Stedfast remarked.

"We do not always succeed," Darien reminded him, "but, praise God, this time we did, we really did."

This couple had been at a crossroads.

If you stay in the area, you will still be influenced by the increasing decadence, by the eroding of all that is good and decent and holy.

That was Darien planting a seed in Bret's mind.

If you go to Colorado Springs, you will be in the midst of a locale that is heading in the opposite direction, toward an expanding spirituality. There you will get much cooperation for your new ministry.

Stedfast was speaking to Molly in that case.

Rather than ignore these promptings, the Erlandsons decided to pay considerable attention.

"We are being guided," Molly said, confident that neither of them was "imagining things."

"I can feel that as well," Bret acknowledged.

Peace.

"I have never before felt as serene as this," Molly spoke, "even a kind of joy, Bret. It's remarkable."

"It is," he replied, "almost as though—"

He did not finish that sentence, hesitating because he did not quite know how to express himself.

"What were you going to say?" his wife prompted him.

"It will sound strange."

Molly was not turned off by that kind of strangeness, not from a man she had loved and trusted for a decade.

"Go ahead, husband," she urged him. "*Be* strange!"

"A voice."

She had not expected that, but it did not disturb her certainly.

"You heard a voice?" she repeated.

"Not that exactly."

"Bret?"

She knew that she had to tell him, now, what happened to her—what she had been confronted with only hours before.

"Yes?" he asked.

He was waiting patiently. Never an arrogant, possessive man, he invariably allowed Molly her "space."

Nevertheless, she felt sheepish, but that did not stop her from admitting to her husband what she had experienced.

CHAPTER 23

"I did as well," Molly finally said, glad to have gotten out in the open what she had kept to herself through the night.

"You—?" he stuttered. "You—?"

Bret's eyes widened, and for a few seconds he could not speak at all, stunned by what she had said.

"You heard a voice?" he was finally able to say.

"Not heard . . . I *felt* it," she tried to explain what may have been unexplainable. "Isn't that odd?"

She threw up her hands in a gesture of frustration.

"I mean, *feeling* something like that instead of hearing it with my ears. After all, that is normal. But this . . . this—!"

He looked at her with great affection.

"That's exactly the way it was with me."

"You felt a voice, too?" she spoke. "Bret, listen to us: How could either you or I *feel* a voice?"

"In our souls."

They were sitting on their front porch, watching the traffic pass by on Shore Road, the busiest of the streets in that section of Linwood, a town that was located just a few miles from Atlantic City.

"How many of the people who go by here day after day ever experience such voices?" Molly mused.

"How many ignore what God is trying to tell them?" Bret added.

"How can we be sure that what was told to us was from God?"

"Satan would not be sending us to Colorado Springs. He would want us to remain trapped here, so close to Atlantic City."

. . . to remain trapped . . . so close to Atlantic City.

They lapsed into silence as they considered the implications of those words. Both had been born and raised in the area. They had many friends nearby. Their church home was just a mile from their house.

And Colorado Springs was so far away.

Yet Bret and Molly knew that Atlantic City was like an alien planet to them anymore. Attitudes were changing.

Gone was any semblance of a small-town mentality in the suburbs.

Strangers kept moving in and eventually took over.

They could no longer be sure of who their neighbors were, with houses being bought and sold as though these were a new form of gambling, investors betting on short-term increases in their value, increases so spectacular that a home worth much less than a hundred thousand three or four years earlier could zoom to four hundred thousand. That sort of fortune-making attracted the boys from Brooklyn and many others, turning the landscape of Atlantic City into one giant crap table.

"What a cornucopia for the Mafia!" exclaimed Bret. "They have it three ways: one, they buy up properties at their depressed prices before gambling starts, then sell these a few years later at five times what they invested, then buy others before the next jump and start the process all over again; two, they skim hundreds of millions of dollars off the take of the casinos through creative accounting that would make the Hollywood studios look like bastions of integrity and ethics by comparison; three, they buy apartment buildings, and raise the rents every so often, citing the mushrooming of taxes, which their gambling interests have been responsible for in the first place."

"The way they do it, they can't lose," Molly speculated.

"Next, with so much money in their coffers, they are able to *own* key local, country, and state officials so well-placed that it sounds like a replay of the 1940s, between Hoover and the mob. And the net spreads wider and wider as more money comes in, safely insulating gangsters from any persecution."

"Wasn't gambling supposed to be free of mob influence *this* time?"

"Look at it this way, Molly: Enough money can corrupt even the most determined of objectives."

"Who isn't on the take?"

"Anyone who can't do the mob any favors. Just about everyone else has sold their soul to these Sicily bullies, either that, or they're stupid enough to believe the propaganda and might as well be bought and paid for!"

"I'm glad—" she started to say.

"Glad?" he repeated.

"Yes, Bret, glad that we're getting out, glad that we can go where the values haven't changed so dramatically for the worst."

He was biting his lower lip.

"What's wrong?" Molly asked.

"I think . . ."

"Think what?"

"I think, in time, you and I could have been corrupted as well."

Her face went white.

"Were you thinking the same thing?" he asked.

She nodded slowly, embarrassed that she was so transparent.

"I had a dream," she spoke, "one in which the two of us ended up on skid row, our children taken away, and given over into the care of strangers, you and I stumbling along in rags, cold, hungry."

"Me, too," Bret acknowledged. "We were ill, and feeling absolutely hopeless, and we decided that we had no reason to go on living."

"Exactly what happened in the dream I had!" Molly exclaimed.

The dream was Darien's idea, not based upon any foreknowledge, since God was the only One who possessed that, but an impression, a hint from the Creator, a concern that Vinnie the Bear would prove too successful in his efforts to get revenge.

"But are they not simply running away now?" Stedfast asked reasonably.

"No, I believe that they are simply showing prudence, and wanting only to be surrounded by those of like belief in an atmosphere that is not so corrosive, so evil."

Evil.

Could that really be said of Atlantic City?

There could be only one answer. Where men like Vincenzo DiCosolo thrived, where the sin of prostitution was experiencing a rebirth, where wickedness in high places could be guaranteed by the love of money buying the souls of men and women, where the elderly have been thrown into the streets because of greed—their own as well as the greed of those who wanted to "upgrade" their apartments into "luxury suites" that were sold, not rented, thereby bringing in many millions of dollars—where all this and more was happening, and yet those in charge of law enforcement, even members of the clergy, were continually looking the other way, or simply sighing as they said, "What can we do? Gambling is here to stay!" could Atlantic City be called evil?

The answer was in another question: Could it be called anything else?

CHAPTER 24

Their last day . . .

"Let's drive along the oceanfront," Bret remarked, recalling wistful visions of years gone by.

"Yes . . ." Molly replied. "That would be nice."

They had spent many hours on the beach between Longport, New Jersey, and Atlantic City. In fact they had ended their first date on a man-made jetty that thrust out into the serene Atlantic Ocean, sitting there on one of the flat chunks of concrete, letting a slight breeze work its way through their hair like gentle fingers.

"So happy then," she recalled with not inconsiderable wistfulness, remembering such moments while knowing that these could never be duplicated again, that they belonged solely to the past, another life, not as in the demonic deception of reincarnation but, rather, simple human experience.

Molly looked at Bret, then their three children who were now sitting next to them, enjoying that moment nearly as much as their parents.

"All these years," Bret mused, "and, now, here we are, turning away and going elsewhere."

"No," Molly told him, "no, I don't look at it like that."

He was puzzled over what his wife meant.

"What other way is there?" he asked. "Or have I missed something here?"

"Atlantic City has turned away from us, you know. People we have known for years are now involved with the casinos at every level, whether as employees, customers, or suppliers. They have bought into this whole thing. And they want little to do with you and me. We represent, in their minds, the extremists trying to stand in the way of their livelihoods and their pleasures."

"And it *will* corrupt them," Bret added. "It can do nothing else."

Something else occurred to Molly.

"Would we be leaving if the kids weren't with us?" she mused.

"I hope so. We put them first in everything, but even if you and I *were* childless, we would probably not remain in this area."

She nodded, smiling a bit.

"You know what?" she asked.

"Go ahead. Tell me."

"We've given the old Atlantic City too much credit. It was never a center for virtuous lifestyles."

"Agreed, but it also didn't act as a beacon for people to come and ruin their lives, either. To do that in the same way, they had Las Vegas. It was what it was—old, antiquated, struggling to survive but not a threat to the morality and the decency of millions of people from so many different states along the East Coast."

The children were becoming restless, eager to begin the long but fascinating drive across country.

"Let's leave via Albany Avenue," Bret suggested.

"Just so you can get one last look at Atlantic City High School," Molly spoke knowingly.

Atlantic City High . . .

Its students had gone on to virtually every profession, including producing movies, which was the case with one of the more fortunate ones, Albert Zugsmith. He worked at Universal Studios and helmed such films as *Written on the Wind, The Incredible Shrinking Man,* and others.

CHAPTER 24

"I was glad to get away from Atlantic City," he said at one point from his later office at the legendary MGM Studios. "There were no opportunities for me there, for many others. It was a dead-end town."

That remark was made by Zugsmith some twenty-five years *before* gambling!

Atlantic City High usually inspired a great deal of affection, and Bret was not immune to this.

"Well, I guess, that's part of it," he acknowledged.

Molly smiled as she said, "Good. That's what we'll do then."

So, the five members of that family got back into their van, and drove the several miles from Longport to Atlantic City where the old building in which both had spent four high school years looked the same as always.

"I think, someday, it will be torn down and a high-rise built in that spot," Bret commented.

"Torn down and replaced," Molly said. "My, that sounds like Atlantic City itself, doesn't it?"

"Sure does."

Nearby, sirens, getting closer . . .

They were about to turn around the traffic circle and head back along Albany Avenue when they noticed two ambulances pull up in front of an apartment building to their right on Pacific Avenue. A squad car joined them seconds later.

"I think—" Bret started to say, a chill working its unwelcome way down his spine.

"What is it?" Molly asked, seeing the expression on his face.

"Those two—"

He swung the van around, cut down one street over, then turned right onto Pacific Avenue.

An available parking meter.

He took the space, and was out of the van in seconds. Molly joined him after she had cautioned the children to stay inside.

Bret approached the small crowd cautiously, almost certain what he would see with horrifying clarity.

And he was right.

Two frail old bodies smashed across the asphalt.

One of them apparently had landed on her face, and then tumbled over on her back somehow, that once wrinkled, pale, vein-lined stretch of aged flesh now nothing more than a grotesque near-shapeless mass of battered, torn skin and protruding bone, the jaw hanging loosely.

The top of the other's head had hit first, cracking open the skull, with brain matter spilling out.

It will be such fun for us. We need some fun in our lives. It's great, that gambling . . .

The arms and legs of both bodies looked like hapless tree limbs caught in a tornado, snapped in an instant, but not broken loose, and twisted at odd angles.

Young people and older ones were turning away in revulsion, with most leaving that spot, unable to endure the sight any longer.

"They would not listen!" Bret exclaimed.

"Only a few did," Molly spoke. "We're fortunate, you and I. And the others who heeded the warnings."

They knew of other couples wise enough to have left months before the first casino opened.

"The most astute of all of us," Bret recalled. "But at least, for you and me and the kids, it's not too late."

Good-bye, the queen of resorts . . .

The Erlandson family left Atlantic City minutes later.

None of them turned and looked back, though both parents were tempted—tempted to glance one last time at the high school and the round columned memorial in the middle of the traffic circle just outside, tempted to hesitate, to reconsider, to give in to natural insecurities. But that was not what they did, instead resisting, for they knew what their Lord wanted them to do, and nothing, nothing, nothing would dissuade them from it.

"I feel peace all of a sudden," Molly told him.

"So do I," Bret replied. "Even though we have no idea, really, what is ahead of us, it's still there, in the center of my soul, a sweet sweet feeling it is."

. . . a sweet sweet feeling it is.

And then they were gone, like the angels assigned to them, embracing the rest of their lives and leaving behind a city symbolized by the splattered bodies of two old women who once believed in the miracle of gambling, which took hold of them and then spat them out, to be scooped up and taken away to the city morgue.

They had no relatives.

Well aware of how active they had been in the pro-gambling movement, other tenants in the same apartment building persuaded the manager to contact the one man who owed them a great deal, and ask for help with the burial costs, since both women were well-nigh penniless by then, and in another week would have been evicted.

Vincenzo DiCosolo never called back.

EPILOGUE

He that plants thorns must never expect to gather roses.

Anonymous

No one told Vinnie the Bear that the Erlandsons had chosen to leave the Atlantic City area.

For some, it was an oversight.

For others, this omission was out of their desire to see Vinnie's downfall, for he had been earning himself enemies since the beginning of his reign.

While he was dealing with cruel and violent men, Vinnie did, ironically, prove to be too ruthless in his own right for them to stomach him much longer.

"To ignore those old women!" Johnny Salvaggio told the council of ten which was comprised of the ruling members of the ten Mafia families across the United States. "Have we become so heartless? They were being kicked out of their apartments. They had no money left. And they committed suicide. *We* stood by and did nothing. Is that what we have become, heartless and cruel?"

Oddly among that group of mobsters were men who could order a massacre but who were little more than piles of Jell-O when it came to the elderly.

"Being old means that you've come just one giant step closer to being buried," Salvaggio reminded them. "Vinnie shows no respect to anyone. I'm sure that he cursed *us* behind our backs!"

That definitely did not sit well with the veteran mob figures at the meeting. Respect was very important to them.

"But you are DiCosolo's lieutenant," one of them said, pointing his finger angrily. "You betray Vinnie. How do we know that, someday, you will not turn around and do the same to us? Can you answer *that,* Johnny?"

Salvaggio was ready for that one.

"Vinnie's behavior betrays us all," he shot back but not in a way that would seem defiant and insulting, a response that would have laid the seeds for his own demise.

"How so?" another don asked.

"Bad press," Salvaggio said. "Bad image, you know. It suggests that we are men without a conscience."

. . . men without a conscience.

To a degree, that was seldom true of the gang lords. Their society was filled with moral and ethical admonitions, rules that instilled a code of behavior that could never be violated without the worst possible consequences.

"I'd have had those little ladies living in such luxury that they would have thought they had already died and gone to heaven!" the same don added, chuckling, and the others joined in with him. "Look at what they helped us to achieve!"

He banged his fist down on the long, solid-wood table around which the group had gathered.

"Vincenzo miscalculated!" he declared. "But has he done anything else?"

"There's more," Salvaggio told him.

That was when he told them about the Erlandsons.

"Revenge?" spoke Frank Muratore. "This character did nothing that was wrong. He stood up for what he believed. He didn't directly try to hurt us. Do we seek revenge against *everyone* who disagrees with us?"

"Apparently Vinnie doesn't feel that way."

"He was going to destroy this man's business, then force him to take a job at one of our casinos?" Muratore asked.

"Either that, or have Erlandson become so impoverished that he would eventually end up on skid row."

"What about the wife, the children?"

"They would have suffered greatly."

"Erlandson was our opponent, not our enemy. Do we not know the difference between the two? I think he is decent. Have we no morality left? Are we becoming what outsiders think we are?"

"As far as Vinnie is concerned, there is no distinction."

"And that is what has spelled his doom, right? Isn't that why we're here now, to do something about it?"

Then another man spoke up.

"Is this all?" he asked. "Or do you have more to give us about Vincenzo?"

Salvaggio knew how solid his "case" was, but he also understood that to appear cocky would have offended the others.

"I have enough for you to think about," he told them, his voice lowered, his tone softer.

"Then tell us," someone said.

He gave them a list of Vinnie's missteps, ranging from ignoring the Atlantic City Rescue Mission's requests for more funds and a long list of others so pervasive that Muratore's mouth dropped open.

"Dignity!" he exclaimed. "What happened to giving this man some dignity? It was an honest fight. He lost, period. That should be the end of it. This isn't some kind of warfare, you know."

He hesitated, then added, "I am shocked. . . . I recommend that we do something about Vincenzo DiCosolo."

It was difficult for two angels, soon to return to heaven, to comprehend any gangster reacting with moral outrage. But that was what they witnessed, showing them a side of the underworld that few outsiders would ever learn about.

"But he has done so much for us," another member of the Council protested, a man not immune to the feeling of gratitude.

"That's right!" Muratore snapped back. "But it's all running along well now. We don't need him. The man's outlived any value he has. Vinnie's a liability now. He has violated too many of our rules. Where would we all *be* without rules? Everyone has to follow these. No one can be excluded."

Vinnie's a liability now. . . .

He never knew in advance what would happen, never guessed that they could have planned what they did, for Vinnie assumed that he was invincible, that the mob would place its gratitude for the countless millions he had enabled them to earn above any short-term mistakes he might make.

But he forgot one of the tenets observed by every don of every family in the United States.

Never harm the elderly.

And, yet, that was what Vinnie the Bear did by ignoring those two old, rather desperate women.

He died the same way, splattered across part of Pacific Avenue just two blocks from where they were found.

And it was not suicide.

Yes, Darien and Stedfast were preparing for their return to heaven when God told the two of them to wait.

"Where are we to go?" Darien asked respectfully but a bit anxiously.

"With the Erlandsons," God informed them both.

"Are they going to need our help?" Stedfast spoke.

"They will. Nor are they the only ones. A new vision, a new insight sweeping the nation. It is going to engulf the gambling interests, as more and more of the real price of gambling becomes known."

"Citizens' groups rising up, Father?" Darien suggested.

"Exactly! There is an open window now, as never before."

"Hallelujah!"

"You should rejoice, yes, my loyal Darien, but the war is not known. The enemy has many weapons."

God paused briefly, then added, "You will be at the forefront of all this."

"Is that why you sent us on this part of our journey?" Stedfast asked.

"It is. You needed to know the facts. You needed to see for yourself. You needed to understand."

As always they saw the wisdom of God, the planning of God, and were inspired by it, emboldened.

"We will do our best," Darien assured his Creator.

"I do not doubt that you will. You will have an increasing number of allies. Real hope springs forth now—real hope that the madness can be stopped, that greed can be shown for what it is, and decent men and women will recoil from it, instead of letting it embrace them."

"A long way to go, Father?"

"A very long way. Gambling cannot be turned back overnight."

They thanked God, and went on their way, ready now—ready to fight the good fight, to reach the very mouth of hell, if necessary, in order to stand between it and the countless numbers of men and women hitching their souls to the spin of a roulette wheel, as their children—spellbound by the neon glitter of it all—awaited their turn.

finis